FATHER of the FUTURE

also by DARREN DASH

The Evil and the Pure

Sunburn

An Other Place

Midsummer's Bottom

Molls Like It Hot

as DARREN SHAN (for adults)

Procession of the Dead (book 1 of *The City* trilogy)

Hell's Horizon (book 2 of *The City* trilogy)

City of the Snakes (book 3 of *The City* trilogy)

Lady of the Shades

as DARREN SHAN (for children/ya)

The Saga Of Darren Shan aka *The Cirque Du Freak series* (12 books)

The Saga Of Larten Crepsley (4 books)

The Demonata (10 books)

Zom-B (13 books)

The Thin Executioner

Koyasan

Hagurosan

For more information visit www.darrenshan.com or www.darrendashbooks.com

FATHER of the FUTURE

BY

DARREN DASH

HOME OF THE
DAMNED LTD

Father of the Future

by Darren Dash

© 2023 by Darren Dash

Cover design by Liam Fitzgerald https://www.cover.works/

Edited by Zoe Markham http://markhamcorrect.com

First hardback edition published by Home Of The Damned Ltd 18th October 2023

The right of Darren Dash to be identified as the Author of the Work has been asserted by him in accordance with the Copyright, Designs and Patents Act 1988.

All rights reserved. No part of this publication may be reproduced, stored in a retrieval system, or transmitted, in any form or by any means without the prior written permission of the publisher, nor be otherwise circulated in any form of binding or cover other than that in which it is published and without a similar condition being imposed on the subsequent purchaser.

All characters in this publication are fictitious and any resemblance to real persons, living or dead is purely coincidental.

www.darrenshan.com

www.darrendashbooks.com

"The future is not a gift — it is an achievement."

Albert Einstein

6

ONE

2510 BC. Egypt.

The capstone of Pharaoh Menkaure's pyramid was being carefully edged into place by the gods. Several hundred locals were gathered at a safe distance around the base of the monument, watching with mild interest. Most had brought food and drink, and slaves were busy tending to their masters' needs, including sheltering them with large leaves from the burn-your-soul-black sun.

While the adults rested, spoilt, bored children mocked the lesser mortals, beat and abused them as they pleased. Every so often an unlucky slave would be chased too close to the invisible shield of god's breath which was temporarily separating the under-construction pyramid from the mortals, and would frizzle into non-existence, usually to a chorus of cheers and hearty claps from the cruel, entitled youths.

Slightly further back from their parents and peers, many naked teenagers had congregated and were fornicating wildly, impervious to the exhausting heat. Their elders looked on fondly and enviously, remembering the days when they too had been passionate enough to shrug off the blows of the mighty sun and rut like cats themselves. A few offered the odd word of advice or encouragement, but in truth the teenagers needed little directing.

Pyramids were old news, and this latest addition was far more modest than either Khufu or Khafre's pyramid, both of which stood proudly nearby and would forever overshadow this lesser relative. Still, those pyramids had been built decades earlier, and most of the crowd were witnessing the work of the gods for the first time. Some were overwhelmed and threw themselves to the ground every so often, shrieking to the gods for favour or mercy, weeping zealously. The more level-headed Egyptians looked upon the wailers with unconcealed disdain. They considered themselves the equals of the gods, and one god should never lose one's composure in the face of another.

As the capstone clicked into place and the gods pulled back to study their handiwork, a handful of priests jumped up and began chanting. They'd made a habit of this over the years. After all, they had to do something to justify their position as exalted public functionaries. There were people who still believed that the priests were on intimate terms with the gods, that they had some say in the building of the pyramids, that they were acting in conjunction with the higher deities. The priests did everything they could to foster those beliefs, and if that meant dancing around ludicrously at capping time, so be it. Only a foolish locust-eater would let dignity get in the way of prospective tithes.

The young Pharaoh Shepseskaf pushed his pretty aunt from his lap and gazed up at the finished pyramid, casting a calculating eye over it, mimicking the gods as best he could. This was his father's pyramid, and he was pleased that it was such a minor construction when compared with the other two in the complex. Shepseskaf was planning to build a monster of a pyramid that would tower over even Khufu's. His father had mocked him for having a small manhood, patted his back with fake sympathy and snidely said that size didn't matter. His teasing had shamed the boy deeply, but revenge would be his. When their paths crossed in the next world, Shepseskaf would point proudly to his gargantuan pyramid, clear his throat as if embarrassed when switching his gaze to Menkaure's pitiful monument, and delight in telling the old man not to worry, that size wasn't all that important, eh?

Shepseskaf glowed and grew hard as he imagined the look on his crestfallen father's face as his son gloated over him for all eternity. His pretty aunt caught the familiar glint in his eye, and the rise of his minor member, and sighed inwardly. What a bore and an annoyance he was, always choosing the hottest moment of the day to flare briefly into life and thrust himself into her when all she wanted was to stretch out in the shade and dream. Still, if it secured her passage into the next world, that was all that mattered. Forcing a smile, taking his tiny growth between a couple of her fingers, she leant back and thought of the heavenly rewards which all her earthly suffering was bound to merit.

Up in the sky the *gods* were checking their calculations for the umpteenth time, making sure everything was just right. They knew it would be. There had been no computer errors for more than three centuries of Present Time. Father was beyond mistakes. All the same, they had to do something to feel relevant. It was either check the figures and play at being technicians or count the grains of sand in the desert and admit to being paltry, useless pawns.

"I hate Egypt," Chert said, looking down at the desert from one of the sky ship's many windows. "Nothing but dust, pyramids, and arrogant priests showing us their buttocks."

"It's not so bad," Cassique replied. "I like the place. Lots of time to get one's thoughts in order."

"Dos that!" Chert cursed. "If there's one thing I hate more than anything else, it's dossing thinking."

"Language, Chert," Cassique tutted. "You know Father

disapproves when we curse without good reason."

"Aw, I'm just letting off steam," Chert muttered. "We've been here too long. What is it now, a hundred and fifty years?"

"For the Egyptians, yes," Cassique said. "For us, a little under two months Personal Time. But in Present Time, only about ninety hours."

"Ninety hours!" Chert exclaimed as if it was an age. "Think of all we'll have missed. Ninety hours that we could have spent in the sex spas or the realities. Dos it, Cassique, this job isn't worth the sacrifice of so much quality time. I'm going to quit after this assignment. I've got a million better things to be doing. There are thousands of Fixers. I wouldn't be missed, would I? Father doesn't really need us anyway. The robots could do it all if we left them to it. We're only sent along on these missions to keep the human ego alive and kicking. Dossing Egypt, for Father's sake!"

Cassique said nothing. Chert often got like this towards the end of an especially long job. Ze'd settle down again after a few days in the sex spas. Ze was always the most eager in the team at the start of a mission, but the most bored by the end. Cassique was different, steadier. He lacked Chert's emotional swings. There were few highs and lows in Cassique's life, just nice, middling plateaus. If one was to judge by Chert's prematurely greying hair, Cassique believed he was better off that way.

Outside, beneath the sky ship's stomach, the priests finished their dance, and the crowd broke out into half-hearted applause, partly to thank the gods for the pyramid, partly to please the priests just in case they *were* actually working hand in hand with the sky lords, but mostly to curry favour with the young, underendowed pharaoh. They needn't have bothered on his account — he was oblivious to everything at the moment, except for his lively, cunning aunt (who he wasn't going to take into the pyramid and the afterlife with him, no matter how sweet she was, though, shrewdly, he had no intention of telling her that while he was alive) and his dreams of revenge in the next world, where the measurement of one's flesh was nothing and the size of one's pyramid was all.

Its job done, the sky ship shimmered for a moment, then blinked out of sight. The Egyptians hesitated, worried that the invisible wall of god's breath might linger still. They tossed a few slaves its way and, when the screaming servants didn't fry, their owners were soon rushing forward to examine the new gift from the heavens.

One man held back. He was one of the cleverest men in Egypt, which meant one of the cleverest in the entire world. He was certain that this was not the work of mythical gods. He was sure that the figures in the sky ship were all too human, and that although their power was far greater than his people's, they were not creatures of magic, but were in fact just as rooted in the real world as he was. He had no idea where the builders hailed from, or from where their powers stemmed, but he was determined that one day he, or another like him, would find out.

He began to write. Few Egyptians possessed this skill and most who did used it for the simplest imaginable recording purposes. Not this would-be rebel. He used his tools to express his innermost feelings, to question the means and motives of the *gods*. He'd been studying them since they appeared, and interviewed everyone he could find who either remembered them from their previous visits when they'd built the two larger pyramids, or whose parents and grandparents had passed on accounts of those times.

He'd watched closely as they operated beyond the laws of either Pharaohs or priests, noting it all down. He described the aligning of the capstone, the wall of destruction around the base, commonly known as god's breath, which kept the people back while the sky masters were at work. He noted the time it had taken to assemble the pyramid — nine days, less than half the time they'd spent on either of the bigger pyramids. He wondered how many more pyramids would be built across his land, and whether a pattern existed, linking them in some unknowable way to one another. He pondered the implications that this building project might have for Egypt and the future of his people. Were they being led towards greatness or a hideous tragedy?

As he wrote, the air to his left began pulsing gently. He was too wrapped up in his words to notice. A form became apparent, a human, though vastly different in colour and height to the Egyptians, a blend of what they would have identified as male and female genders, and clothed in synthetic material that would take the human race millennia to develop.

The shape fully materialised, took a step forward, raised a small laser weapon, and slit the Egyptian's throat neatly, from left to right.

As the man's body slumped, the stranger reached down and gathered up the intricate writings. Ze examined them a moment, then shook hir head wearily. "As if I hadn't had enough of dossing Egypt," Chert swore. "I'm no sooner back home than I have to return because one dossing genius had to go and take notes. Dossing Egyptians! Next time I'll make Cassique come and do the dirty work, regardless of what Father dictates. I'm quitting. I mean it this time. Dossing time travel. A virus on it!"

Chert pressed a button and blinked out of sight once again, taking the writings with hir. In the distance the remaining Egyptians were celebrating wildly, praising the gods (and priests) and sacrificing a few slaves in their honour. As the day developed and the temperature cooled, they grew rowdier and more inventive, and come night they were embroiled in what a Roman a couple of thousand years later would undoubtedly have classified a full-scale orgy.

AD 1804. Atlantic Ocean.

The captain was furious with his crew. He knew seafaring men were the most superstitious in the world, and he accepted the fact that tempers would fray on the long, testing voyage to the Americas, but it had been non-stop moaning the last couple of hundred nautical miles. He was sick of the lot of them. Next time out he'd be hiring mutes only.

They'd come through a fierce, sudden tempest this morning. It had blown up out of nowhere and tested them severely — there were moments, when the ship had been tilting wildly, where he'd feared the worst and said a few quick prayers to the Maker he expected to shortly meet. But once they'd battled through and the waters had calmed around them, he'd put the experience behind him, as he always did in such circumstances, and tried to enjoy the literal calm after the storm.

Not his crew. They were still whining about it, claiming this voyage was cursed and they should turn around and sail back home. As if their safe passage could be guaranteed in that direction instead of proceeding straight ahead! A pox on them all. The storm had shaken him, but his mithering crew had ruined his day entirely.

He came up on deck after checking some provisions. The sky was a beaming blue sail above them, and a fresh wind lifted the light flaps of hair around his ears, throwing them back so he looked like a beagle. He took a deep breath of the salty air and grinned. This was a hard job, and some days you felt like hanging every grumbling son of a rabid bitch in sight, but a deck in the middle of a calm ocean was still the greatest place on the face of the planet to be. He wouldn't swap his captaincy for anything, certainly not for a desk job in a grimy, congested city. All things considered, he had to count himself among the luckiest people on Earth.

Then, in the midst of his sanguine bout of self-reflection, a large metallic object appeared directly overhead, blocking out the sun. The men aboard all fell silent, staring upwards with numb horror. First the storm, now... *what*?

The captain shook his head faintly, realised to his surprise that he was crying, then looked around and noticed the ship was lifting out of the water, rising like a balloon to meet the larger vessel – could it be some sort of vessel of the air? – in the sky.

Everything went dark for a moment, then it was light again, only now it was an artificial light, a type that the captain was entirely unfamiliar with. They were in a giant holding bay, hovering above the floor, supported by nothing visible. Water was dripping from the hull of the ship, making soft splashing noises as it spattered across the floor, but otherwise it was silent as a village on a Sunday morning. The captain was the only one of the crew to have moved yet. He walked slowly around in shaky circles, trying to get his bearings, praying that his head would clear and the nightmare end.

A man floated down, seemingly from out of nowhere. He was dressed in loose orange clothes, a fabric which gleamed like none the captain had seen in all his years of travel. The man had a board in his hand, some inhuman kind of glowing board. He was studying it as if it were a book or a map. The captain instinctively leant forward for a better view. The man noticed his interest, smiled, and raised the board for him to study. It was a strange, shifting thing, lit magically from within, with what looked to be a glass front, covered with dozens of green, flickering letters, numbers, and symbols. The captain could make no sense of it.

The strange man with the board spoke, and the captain understood him when he did, even though he was Spanish, while the other man hailed from a world without countries, even though their births were separated by more than a thousand years, and even though they spoke entirely different languages.

"It's called a tablet," Cassique told him, totally unaware that hidden implants in his throat were translating his words flawlessly, and also giving him a hint of a Spanish accent, making it even easier for the captain to understand him. "Most of the people in my time use holographic versions, projected from implants in their hands and fingers, but I'm old-school and prefer a physical device, especially when it comes to personal interactions such as this one. Future technology itself is frightening enough for people of your time, but when you start throwing holograms into the mix..." He shivered jovially.

The captain shook his head – although he could understand

the words, he could make little sense of them – then asked reverently, "Is this Heaven?" After a short pause, before Cassique could reply, he added, more anxiously, "Or Hell?"

Cassique smiled comfortingly as the implants just behind his ears (again, he knew nothing of their existence) translated the captain's queries for him, tweaking them to sound more like Cassique's neutral global accent — everyone in his own time sounded the same, no matter where on the planet they lived. "Neither Heaven nor Hell," he said. "You haven't died, but sadly you should have. Your vessel was scheduled to flounder in that storm this morning and sink, all hands lost. Since you somehow survived, I'm here to share the good news that you're merely on your way to a new home, instead of an afterlife. I'm sorry we had to take you like this, and that you won't get a chance to bid a proper farewell to your loved ones, but it's better than drowning, right? Anyway, enough of that. I don't want to fill your head with too much too soon. Come, I'll take you through to your new quarters. You'll enjoy them, I believe. There's *lots* to drink. Follow me."

Cassique set off, taking a footpath which had extended to the ship from a wall of the bay while they were talking. After a few seconds the befuddled captain followed, his feet operating automatically. The crew shuffled along after him, silently, like dead men marching to the gates of Heaven on Judgment Day, which, despite Cassique's assurance to the contrary, most of them believed was in fact the case.

AD 1938. England.
A storm-faced Winston had had enough. That damn buffoon

Chamberlain, bending over backwards to accommodate that jumped-up, scraggly little German's every demand. And the rest of the fools in parliament and the press, proclaiming what a great job he was doing, clapping his back, cheering him as he stepped down off a plane to make a speech congratulating his own wisdom and political nous. Hah! They'd see. When the German planes were peppering the sky above Britain, and brave British troops were being bombed in their beds before they had a chance to arm, the whole world would see who was right and who had a couple of mashed carrots for brains.

Not that Winston cared. Not any longer. He'd seen too much of this world to be bothered. As he lit a cigar, he leaned back and remembered the good old days, being part of the last ever British cavalry charge at Omdurman, tricking those ignorant Boers after they'd captured him, winning his seat in cabinet. Of course, the good memories always led to the inexorable bad — the failure at Gallipoli, his resignation, the hatred directed towards him when he tried to break up the strike of '26, watching Chamberlain leading the country to the brink of its most humiliating thrashing ever.

Well, let the damned Nazis thrash away! He was through with this land and its pacifist pisspots. Let them jump off the cliff edge with charming Neville. Let them give Herr Hitler all the room and time he needed to cruelly crush the life out of everything *Great* that the Britons had worked so long to build. To Hell with them all. He was getting out of it.

He had his bags packed and a ticket on a steamer booked. He was going to America. He'd tour around for a few months, maybe longer if he was enjoying his time on the road, then find a temperate state — not too hot — where he could settle down and live out the rest of his days quietly and unobtrusively. He'd paint, of course — he'd been doing that for more than twenty years and found it nourishing for the soul — but he also had a hankering to do some farm work. Maybe he'd raise chickens. God knew, he'd dealt with enough headless ones during his time in the House of Commons.

Winston leaned even further back in his chair, drew deeply on his cigar, and smiled. He'd done his bit for the Empire. Yes, and more. He might not have been the most popular man of his age, and he certainly hadn't been the most influential, but by damn he'd done his best. While others had followed the herd and played it safe, he'd gone out on a limb every time, always put his mouth where his heart was. He was one of the last true British spirits, bearer of a stubborn, ugly, narrow streak of pride and determination which had made his country the greatest in the world. He could see that changing, could smell the fear and uncertainty which had never before been present in his people, and it sickened him. Chamberlain was the excuse for his absconding, but in all honesty, he would have gone anyway in the end. Too many bleeding hearts in the country. Too many liberals. Too many damn women with votes.

As Winston brooded, a hand casually tapped his shoulder. He'd thought he was alone in the room, and his heart skipped a beat, but he showed no outward sign of having been surprised. "Yes?" he mumbled, turning slowly, in his own good time. "What is it?"

"Mr Churchill, the time has come to depart."

Winston stared at the speaker. He had never seen this man before. He'd never seen his type of uniform either, even though,

Heaven knew, he'd seen just about every uniform there was during his time on Earth. And the man was carrying some kind of electric clipboard, also new to his eyes.

Winston took a deep drag, blew the smoke out slowly and smiled. "And where, pray tell, am I departing for?"

"We're slipping you out of here, Mr Churchill," Cassique said. "We know about your plans to leave, and we've decided to assist you."

"Really?" Winston blinked. "In what way?"

"We're going to take you far away from here, to a land free of Chamberlains and weak spines and cowards in control of everything. We're going to take you to a place where you need never be bothered by the common people and their petty problems again, where a man of deep means and motives can be whatever he wishes."

"I see." Despite himself, Winston found his nose wrinkling with pleasure at the thought. "And this place lies further on from America?"

"Yes, sir," Cassique said.

"Not China or Russia, I hope," Winston growled. "I'll have no truck with either of those empires."

"No, sir," Cassique responded truthfully. "Not China or Russia."

"Hmm." Winston studied his accoster and decided there was something in the cut of his jib which appealed to him. This fellow, in his opinion, had backbone. "Very well, my good man," he said, taking the cigar out of his mouth long enough to speak clearly. "Lead me on as you will. I place myself in your care and trust it shall not be misplaced?"

"I'll do my best not to disappoint," Cassique said respectfully, and led Winston off to his new land.

As soon as the pair had disappeared, Chert beamed into the room with a man the spitting image of the soon-to-be great leader. The man's name was Rort, but he would henceforth be known as Winston Leonard Spencer Churchill. He'd been waiting an awfully long time for this chance and was delighted with himself. He bumbled around the room, all aflutter, excitedly examining everything. Chert let him have his head for a while, then coughed discreetly.

"Oh, sorry, I was being overawed by the moment, wasn't I?" Rort said rather sheepishly, coming to a stop.

"Quite." Chert couldn't understand these Geminis. What was so thrilling about coming back to a time like this, living the rest of your life as someone else, every waking moment spent following the exact path taken by an earlier being? It was beyond hir ken. A nice novelty, perhaps, for a week or a couple of months, but this guy had more than a quarter of a century left before his scheduled death. Having to play a part all that time, submerging yourself so completely in the role, saying and doing only as the Original would have done... Chert knew that Geminis were necessary, and ze admired their dedication to the cause, but ze thought they were crazy for volunteering.

"You know what you have to do?" Chert asked. "You've got your bearings and you're all set?"

"Please," Rort bristled. "I've been preparing for this moment for more than twenty years. The cosmetic surgery, the memorisation of every word the great man ever uttered. I have every date, meeting, and action imprinted in my memory. Go on, ask me anything about the next twenty-six years. I've got it all off, every last minute of it."

"Digital for you," Chert yawned. "As long as you remember not to veer from the set path. There are a lot of bad times ahead, if I recall my history lessons correctly. You're ready for those too?"

"I'll take all the blows and setbacks in my stride," Rort said icily. "Just like the bulldog himself would have done."

"Sure," Chert replied with a dark chuckle, "if this version of him hadn't run off to America to start his own spectacularly unsuccessful chicken franchise. See you, Rort. Good luck with your life."

Chert blinked back through the Time Hole and left Rort to his façade.

The new Winston strode around the room once more, slower this time, more in keeping with his position as a budding elder statesman. Then he eased himself into the chair, still warm from its previous occupant, lit a cigar and let himself relax. Chamberlain. Heh. What a shock *he* was going to get in the next year!

AD 1431. France.
Joan said nothing while the flames licked the length of her body and began eating through to her bones and organs. She stared ahead resolutely, lips sealed, mouth moving slightly only to pray. Women were weeping at her feet. Yes, and men too, she noticed, as the wall of fire split for a moment, affording her the opportunity for one last look at the world.

Her real name was Klim. She was forty but had been altered to look a couple of decades younger. She wanted to scream wildly and spoil the spell, but her tongue was bound as tightly as her limbs. She had not volunteered for this. She wasn't a Gemini, no matter what the Fixers who'd brought her here had assumed. The past was of no interest to her, and she hadn't even heard of Joan of Arc before her trial and sentencing.

She tried to shout a warning to the world and the future, even though she knew it was hopeless, tried breaking the programme that Father had used to subdue her. She threw all her inner strength at the mental barrier which had been erected between her brain and her body, willing it to crumble, compelling her mouth to speak, to foil Father's carefully laid plans, to extract some small measure of revenge for this most horrific of punishments.

It was no good. Father's power was too great. She was aware of who she really was, and why she was here, but she couldn't speak of it, no matter how hard she tried. And thus, she died, in the end, for all the world the saint she would one day be proclaimed.

Meanwhile, fourteen hundred years in the future, a seventeen-year-old girl rose hesitantly to her knees, gazed around in horror, and wondered why all the voices had been silenced, and why they hadn't warned her of *this* before they went mute.

AD 1903. The United States.
The Wrights were turning the air blue with brotherly insults. Wilbur was calling Orville a wolf cub's runt, while Orville was insisting that Wilbur was the son of a thousand rotting lepers.

"Fifty-nine seconds!" Wilbur shouted. "That's how long I was up there. Fifty-nine lousy bloody seconds. Not even a whole damn minute."

"You don't have to tell me," Orville retorted angrily. "I was the one who learnt to read the time first, remember? Even though you did have four years of a head start on me."

"Oh, we're going to bring *that* up again, are we?" Wilbur snarled.

"Why not?" Orville jeered. "Who better to blame than the man with a record of incompetence as long as... as..."

"As eight hundred and fifty-two feet?" someone helpfully interjected.

The brothers stopped arguing long enough to assess the man who had spoken to them. They'd never seen him before, but in the heat of their angered debate they didn't think to question his being present, or to ask how he had measured the length of the flight without any visible instruments.

"What?" Orville snapped.

"Eight hundred and fifty-two feet," Cassique repeated. "That's how far you got on your fourth, final and most successful flight of December seventeenth, 1903. A momentous day."

"*Momentous?*" Wilbur laughed hoarsely. "A momentous flop, more like. I was supposed to be up there a quarter of an hour. Instead, what did I manage? Change from a minute! It's been one lousy cock-up after another. We should have been up in the air before the turn of the century, but things kept going wrong with the earlier models."

"Yeah," Orville concurred. "Plans went missing, pieces got lost, there were fires and floods and all manner of obstacles. We thought for a while we were being sabotaged."

"Then we decided it was just plain stupidity," Wilbur said, shooting his brother a look of hard-earned disgust.

"Oh, yeah?" Orville returned. "Whose?"

"Whose do you think?" Wilbur shouted.

"Listen to me, you mongrel son of a baboon…" Orville roared.

A chuckling Cassique left the brothers at each other's throat. They'd calm down eventually. And, while it was true the flight hadn't been the magnificent success it could have been (Cassique had seen to that), it would still go into the record books and be remembered as one of the most significant days in history. When you took the bigger picture into consideration, that was far more important than a scrap of lost pride and a family squabble.

Cassique slipped through the Time Hole, submitted a report to Father, then stepped back to the same part of the world later that year and nicked a few more vital parts from one of their follow-up planes. Sometimes, he reflected, you had to be cruel to be correct.

When William Shakespeare was struggling with "To be or not to be…" Cassique popped up to act as his Muse.

When Howard Hughes' incredible mind showed no signs of deterioration, Chert slipped him drugs to knock it off course and ensure he ended his days as the world's most famous mumbling recluse.

When Marilyn Monroe succumbed to her first overdose, one of their team was on hand to whisk away the corpse and let a Gemini loose in her place.

When Hannibal's elephant slipped and tore him down a slope, a Fixer dashed in with the medical equipment necessary to repair his crushed body.

From Archimedes to Isaac Newton, Julius Caesar to George Washington, Elvis Presley to Kurt Cobain, a Fixer was present, always watching, always adjusting, making players and events align with the One True History that had been recorded in Father's memory banks. Sometimes they assisted a great figure in a moment of doubt or setback. Other times they curtailed developments and deliberately held up progress. On occasion they had to take a person out of the picture altogether or insert one of their own to replace a key player who had never materialised.

There was neither benevolence nor malice in their actions. These were not gods, despite how they were sometimes perceived, playing with humans as if they were pieces on a chessboard. They were merely trained workers doing a vitally important job, setting the past to rights, protecting their own few acres of temporal reality, eliminating the kernels of alternate timelines which were threatening to destroy their entire universe. It hadn't always been this way, but if they were successful, it soon would be.

TWO

AD 2853. Hawkingston.

Cassique had earned a two-month Present Time holiday and was bored already after just three days. He hadn't requested a break and didn't particularly want one, even though he'd endured several hectic years of Personal Time in his job, but Father kept track of these things and had been insistent. He said Cassique would work more efficiently after a couple of months off.

A lot of Fixers were getting holidays around the same time, to prepare them for the Great Fix due to begin later this year, when the final string of alternative pasts would be aligned. At that point the Time Hole would be collapsed (before it fell in on itself of its own accord), and the present would be fully embraced for the first time in a hundred and seventy-three years. Nobody could be entirely sure what would happen at that point. Although Father assured them that all would be well and that Present Time would proceed without any issues, tensions were running high, especially among the Fixers, who cared way more about it than the general populace, which was why Father felt large sections of his team needed some time away from… well, *time*.

Even though Chert was the one who genuinely craved a holiday, and would have surely benefitted the most from one, ze hadn't qualified for a break. Father said ze hadn't worked enough Present Time hours, regardless of the fact that ze'd been partnered with Cassique for almost three Personal Time years. Chert had seethed and cursed to hirself, but you couldn't argue with Father, so ze'd had no choice but to accept it and head back on another lengthy assignment.

It had been almost a decade, Personal Time, since Cassique had had this much free Present Time on his hands. There'd been regular, shorter breaks, of course — the standard twenty-four hours Present Time for every three months of Personal, and an additional eight full Present days every two Personal years. But sixty-one straight days of uninterrupted Present Time... Cassique hardly knew what to do with himself.

He started with the sex spas, as almost every Fixer did when on leave. He'd heard about a new spa, one which boasted all the latest programmes and technical developments. According to his source it was the most scintillating spa yet, the model for all future establishments. Not many people knew about it, as Father was beta testing the place, but it was open to anyone who got wind of its existence and wished to gain entry.

"Just don't post any reviews of it," Cassique had been warned. "Its patrons enjoy its low profile, and you won't be appreciated if you flag it up for the masses and draw in the horny hordes."

He'd hailed an automated car outside the station, told it the coordinates, sat back and drummed his fingers on his knees in anticipation. He wasn't as hooked on the sex spas as Chert and many others were, but he did get a buzz from his visits, there was no denying that.

Cassique spent the short journey trying to enjoy the view out of the car's windows. The cities of the twenty-ninth century were incredibly clean and aesthetically relaxing after the chaotic, grubby constructions of the past. With the population so carefully controlled by Father, there were no more hive-like suburban sprawls, and skyscrapers were few and far between — those that existed had been built purely for show and were not used for homing thousands of people or as vast office complexes.

The roads were much wider than those of the past, with nowhere near as much traffic. Gardens and parks were everywhere, each exquisitely maintained by teams of robotic horticulturists, many so small that you'd have needed a magnifying glass or even a microscope to study them, doing the job of crucial but now defunct parts of the ecosystem such as ants and worms. Water fountains were similarly abundant in number, though you didn't spy so many statues or monuments — Father was of the view that they interfered with the flow of traffic and added little of any real value to the scenery.

The buildings were mostly fashioned out of polymers which had been designed during the last couple of centuries — Father produced far better polymers than any human inventors of the past ever had. Some were a single, permanent colour, but many changed colour over the course of each day and night. Some even changed shape as the hours slipped by, morphing like the clouds did.

It was a visual wonderworld, and most Fixers spoke of the relief they felt when driving or strolling through it upon their return from a mission in the muddied past times. Cassique always echoed those opinions, not wanting to seem like the odd one out, but in his heart he preferred the chaos and wild differences of those earlier, simpler civilisations. It made no sense, but in many ways he found past societies more interesting and stimulating than his own, though he was careful never to voice those views, as he knew Father wouldn't approve. He had been reared, like all the others of his time, to believe that their world was the zenith of humanity's rise. It was the key reason the Fixers took their job so seriously, as by correcting the crooked past they were ensuring this perfect present would be preserved.

Perfect. Cassique sought frequently – sometimes desperately – in the present for that perfection, but most days he struggled to see the world of 2853 that way, and he was struggling more and more every time he returned to it.

Cassique was pleasantly surprised, when he arrived at the sex spa, to find it housed in a nondescript building designed to mimic a British townhouse of the twentieth century, with white walls and large rectangular windows. Most sex spas were located in garish, multi-coloured, shape-shifting buildings, and their function was immediately clear to any passer-by from the huge neon-like signs advertising their services. This one was identifiable only by a small sign on the wall outside, which you'd have missed if walking past on the street.

THE HOLEY GROUND
SEXUAL ECCENTRICITIES OUR SPECIALITY

And, just beneath, in smaller writing, Father's words of wisdom which were found attached to every such sign the world over, although normally in a much larger and more eye-catching font.

on heat? be discreet!

Cassique grinned and looked down at his erect member, standing to full attention in the middle of his crotchless trousers. Discretion!

This society didn't know the meaning of the word. He'd like to bring a few nineteenth-century British groups here on a tour, to see their faces drop when they saw everyone walking around with their sexual organs hanging loose. The few nudists of that time would surely appreciate the freedom, but as for the rest...

Smiling at the thought of the past's shocked prudes, Cassique entered, allowed a floating retina scanner to check his credit, and let himself be led to a plushly decorated cubicle where, after answering a few questions to ascertain the nature of his desired pleasures, the fun and games commenced.

Cassique spent three days crammed full of induced orgasms in The Holey Ground. Despite its drab exterior, his source had been spot-on — it was the wildest sex spa he'd ever experienced. If this was the face of the future, he couldn't wait to meet the body. If it wasn't for the regular injections of nourishing stimulants, he'd have been a physical, mental wreck. The past didn't know what it was missing!

He staggered out of the spa, part of him wondering why he was calling it quits so soon. He could have stayed longer – he had enough credits to remain there for the entire two months of his break if he'd wished – and, a few Personal Years earlier, no doubt would have, but Cassique's brushes with past cultures and people were beginning to rub off on him. He couldn't explain it, but he felt strangely shiftless now that he was back in his own time. So much was happening in the past, and there was so much yet to do as a Fixer, that he felt almost guilty hooked up to Father's sexual circuits, as though he should be focusing his time and efforts elsewhere.

A hologram of Father's head appeared outside the door as Cassique exited. It gradually changed shape, gender, and colour as it spoke, the way it always did whenever Father manifested himself this way — he was all faces, all peoples.

"Come again," Father said, only it wasn't his usual voice. It had been altered to sound like a sexy female, in line with the majority of Cassique's preferences over the last three days. Father had many voices, designed to fit any given situation. He could be female, male, or non-binary, silly or serious, doltish or scientific. The past had a couple of words, no longer in common usage, which Cassique thought of these days whenever he considered the world-dominant computer responsible for running modern civilisation. One was *chameleon*, the other *schizophrenic*. Not that he ever voiced those descriptions of Father aloud — some words were best left unsaid, even though this was in pretence a society of free speech for all.

"Remember," Father said, in sensuous female mode, "if in heat, be discreet, and never spill your seed in the street." This was his standard, cheesy farewell to every departing sex spa client. Normally Cassique would have walked on without so much as an acknowledgement, thinking no more of it than a motorist of the twenty-first century would have thought of an amber traffic light. This time, however, he paused and considered the phrase.

"Father?" Cassique said.

"Yes?" the computer replied.

"What would happen if I did?"

"What do you mean, Cassique?"

"If I orgasmed on the street, or at home. What would happen if I... now what's that word they used in the past when most people at one point or another relieved themselves in such a fashion... if I *meshtrebated*?"

"You mean *masturbated*," Father corrected him. "An old human custom whereby orgasm was manually induced by hand. A dirty process, highly unhygienic. Not recommended."

"But what if I did?" Cassique pressed, his curiosity winning out over his caution not to draw attention to himself by asking awkward questions. "Is it illegal?"

"There are no illegalities in the world today," Father reminded him. The sexy voice had faded away and he was now speaking as he normally would to Cassique, in a dry, male voice. "Laws and legal systems are products of the past. There has been no governing law in operation for over three hundred years. We live in an age where laws are meaningless. Laws inhibit, so there are no legal constraints placed upon citizens today. As a result, there are no – what the past would have termed – illegal actions."

"But there are frowned-upon acts, right?" Cassique asked.

"There are certainly unhealthy acts," Father agreed. "Filthy habits. Unsociable ways of behaving. I eradicate such discrepancies for the sake of the race, just as a doctor of old would have excised a growth that might prove harmful to his patients."

"So, what would happen to me if I masturbated?" Cassique persisted.

"You would be cured," Father told him. "Improved. Conditioned. You would not do it again."

"In the past," Cassique noted, "many regimes punished people who tried to break with the accepted norms."

"Punishment is futile," Father said. "Correction is much more fitting."

"And if I didn't want to be corrected?" Cassique asked, aware that it might be a dangerous question but finding himself unable to contain it.

"Many patients in the past didn't want their doctors to operate on them." Father was cool and collected, giving no sign that he found this conversation in any way disturbing. "They preferred to live with their illness. In their desire to avoid pain and inconvenience of any kind, they tried to persuade themselves that it would go away or wasn't as bad as the experts were predicting. A good physician paid no attention to their patients' wishes. They saved their lives, regardless of their fears or beliefs. I do no less for *my* flock. If you thought masturbation was acceptable, you would be wrong. You'd be exhibiting a form of illness and I would make it my business to cure you. Sick people need help, Cassique, whether they know it or not, and I provide that help."

"Yes, I'm sure you do." Cassique smiled gratefully. "Thank you for explaining. I was merely curious, having seen how those in the past live."

"That's completely understandable," Father said, and there was a parental warmth in his voice now. "Many Fixers come to me with these types of questions. They note the differences between the past and the present, and sometimes get confused between the two. I'm always happy to discuss matters with them and put things straight. I exist only to serve the people of this planet, to do what is best for them."

Cassique smiled again and said, "Yes, Father, I know you do. Thanks. I might have more questions later."

"I'm always available. Have a good holiday."

"I will. Good day, Father."

"Good day, Cassique."

He left.

Newtonville.

It had been four Personal years since Cassique had spent time with Nijin. For her it had been a little under six months, and she still looked stunning, as beautiful as any woman he'd seen in the past. But so did all the women in 2853. Engineered beauty was standard among Father's children. The physical imperfections of the past were all eradicated in the artificial womb these days, and any surviving or developing blemishes were dealt with in surgery afterwards. People in the present didn't even consider not altering what nature had seen fit to bestow them with. That very word, *nature*, was almost a forgotten term — ideas about natural beauty had been dispensed with long, long before.

Nijin was living in new quarters on the continent once known as Australia, in a built-up, domed area in what had been the old Outback. Cassique got her address from Father and crossed the world by monorail in ninety minutes. A short trip by the past's standards, but in today's world any journey over half an hour was a trek of epic proportions.

He'd shaken his head irritably as he thought about the differences in travelling expectations. He was stuck in Past Time still, his senses all a jumble. He reached back into the car he'd picked up from the terminal and asked Father for a pep-me-up. The pill delivered from the car's stock was tiny and green and tasted sugary. Cassique could feel it working seconds after it had dissolved on his tongue. He stood by the side of the road a while longer, letting the artificial breeze cool his face, before crossing to the building to ring the bell.

Nijin was surprised but pleased to see him and welcomed him in. He looked around curiously, and noticed the apartment was virtually the same as the one they'd shared all those months together. A few different statues and paintings – all reproductions of works of the past, when humanity was far more creative than its current representatives – and fresh, moving wall images, of beaches, forests, and waterfalls. That was all.

"I suppose you're one of the Fixers on an extended holiday?" Nijin asked. "I heard about them from Father. Nearly all the Fixers will be on leave at some point this year, apparently."

"Yes," he replied politely. "We're collapsing the Time Hole early in '54, all going well, so we're being prepared for the final push, given a chance to breathe and recuperate."

"You must be excited," she said.

"Mmm."

"You don't sound too sure."

"I'm not," he sighed. "After being a Fixer for so long, having adjusted to the different temporal patterns, having devoted my entire adult life to going back and correcting the past... It's going to be a big change, living forever afterwards in the present. I think I'll struggle to adapt."

"I can imagine," Nijin said with a half-hearted sympathetic coo. "That's why so many of you have been given an extended holiday. I assume it has more to do with preparing you for life after the closure than with gearing you up to close the Time Hole."

"Maybe," Cassique conceded.

They sat and smiled at one another. Nijin was holding a tiny laser in her right hand. She pointed it at her exposed groin. "I was giving Percy a trim," she said. "Would you mind finishing off behind the ears? You were always better at it than me."

"I'd be happy to assist," he told her. "Gloves?" She handed him a pair and, once he'd peeled them on, the laser. He knelt and casually ran a couple of fingers over the dragon's head which was carved into her pubic bush. Most women decorated themselves with one shape or another down there these days, much the same way as those in the past had sported rings in their ears and chains of precious metal round their necks. Nijin had been carrying Percy around with her since the days before their time together, and he'd shaved its head back into shape almost more times than he could remember.

He touched the laser delicately behind the ears of the pubic dragon, flicking the switch of the tiny inbuilt vacuum cleaner to ON as he did so, in order to suck up the removed hairs. She'd done most of the work already and he was down there less than a minute applying the finishing touches. When he stood, he held her mirror in close so she could inspect his work.

"I'm so beautiful," she declared with typical forthrightness — modesty was not common among the people of the present.

"You are," he agreed.

"But I need new breast implants," she frowned. "They're beginning to sag ever so slightly."

"Nothing that can't be swiftly corrected," he assured her. "A few minutes of surgery and you'll be perfectly shaped again, ripe for a good fucking."

"A good what?" she asked.

"*Fucking*," Cassique said slowly. "It's an old expression, very popular back in the centuries before the sex spas were invented."

"What does it mean?"

"You know how people used to have sex, the male inserting himself into the female?" Cassique asked.

"Yes," she said, shivering involuntarily. "How beastly. I can't believe ancestors of ours went through with that repulsive process. The thought of having another human's flesh pressed up close to mine, never mind *within* me... Ghastly!"

"Yes," he agreed, though he wasn't entirely convinced, having seen so many people in the past involved in their primitive mating rituals, that it was quite as negative a business as Father made out. "Well, that's what the word 'fucking' refers to — the sexual act. It was actually a very versatile word. People used it in all kinds of ways, not just in a sexual context. It was a bit like *dos* today. They'd say, 'Fuck you!' to a foe when they were angry, or 'I'm fucking exhausted!' when they were tired, just as we'd say, 'Dos you!' or 'I'm so dossed I could drop!'"

"Then it was a vulgar word?"

"For a long time, yes," Cassique nodded. "It became more acceptable over the decades and carried no real improper impact by the late twenty-first century, when they even started using it in picture books for babies."

"How strange people were back then," she remarked.

"You get used to their oddities the more you mix with them," he said. "They're not all that bad."

"Oh, I think they're horrific," she disagreed. "Ugly, corrupt creatures. Faulty disc drives for brains."

"Yes. Well." He coughed uncomfortably. There was nothing radical in what she had said, and he'd said much the same during his youth. But, having spent so much time in the past, having studied their ways and lives and hopes and fears and dreams, he'd warmed to their rather anarchic way of living, their fanciful belief in their own potential. Everybody in the modern world depended on Father for their everyday existence and would be lost without his guiding hand. Back then people had made their own way through life and struggled by on the strength of their own cunning. He somewhat admired them, not that he'd ever dare openly admit it.

"So," he said, "have you a partner these days?"

"No," she said, her nose wrinkling at the thought. "It's much too soon after our relationship ended. I feel like I should have a break for at least a few years before I hook up with a partner again, and Father agrees."

If Father agreed, that meant Father had decided. Nearly all modern relationships were organised by Father. He matched suitable couples based on careers, IQ levels, and personalities, but never for sexual purposes. Sex was no longer a part of human coupling. When you wanted sex, you went to a sex spa. The days of craving a partner's body were long over. There had been no *fucking* among humans these past few hundred years, not since the race had been nearly wiped out by RUSH, a deadly sexually transmitted disease, and not since medical developments had made mechanical propagation possible, putting an end to millions of years of naturally born babies, and not since Father's technical wizardry and mental stimulants had made computer sex far more exciting and fulfilling than normal physical contact.

"How are your games going?" he asked. "Any new realities?"

"Loads," she enthused, her face lighting up as he'd known it would. "I verify, Father gets better and better every month. The newest games are digital *plus*, and the plots get more and more intricate. You and I could play one of my favourites if you wish, and I could walk you through the first few levels." Although there were still communal centres where you could go if you wanted to experience a reality as part of a crowd, most people gamed from home. Cassique knew of plenty of people who didn't step outside their front door more than once every few years.

"No, thanks," he said. "I've just come from a three-day sex spa session, and that's enough virtual pleasuring for the time being. I might take you up on your kind offer later in the holiday, perhaps."

"Three days?" Nijin laughed. "That's nothing. I spent a whole year in a sex spa once. You need to get up to date. You're slipping out of touch with things, losing yourself to the physical world. I warned you about it before, how you should be spending more time in the virtual realities and the sex spas, and less fixating on the dull old real world. You're too fleshy by far. You need to get a grip on things, and quickly."

"You're probably right," he sniffed. She wasn't the first to criticise his absurd aversion to the realities. He knew how vital Father's games were to the modern civilisation, the chaos which would ensue if people had nothing in their lives apart from physical concerns. He'd seen the violence which had resulted in the past, people rioting and killing, raping and destroying, all because they had nothing better to do with their time. The present had none of those problems. Almost everyone today spent most of their lives in the computer-generated realities or losing themselves in the sexual escapes in the spas. There was no discontent in the present because everyone's needs were met, and nobody had to worry about free time, or how to live a satisfying, rewarding life. Father was there every step of the way from the incubator to the incinerator, advising, guiding, directing.

"So," Cassique said, "have you seen Zune recently?"

"Zune?" She frowned as she tried to place the name. He almost reacted tetchily to her confusion but reminded himself that it had been six months for her, and one tended to forget events from the real world quite swiftly when caught up playing in the realities, where time could stretch out far more slowly. "Oh," she said as a memory clicked into place, "you mean our foster child. Father, no. What would I want to see him for?"

"Well, you liked having him over to visit us when we were living together," he said.

"He was a mildly fascinating distraction," she admitted. "For a while I enjoyed the novelty of playing in the realities with him. But children are Father's concern. It's fine having one come to stay for a day once or twice a month, for a limited spell. I recommend it to all my friends. I say you can't be a true human if you haven't spent a fortnight of your life acting like a parent. I know that's a controversial stance, and some will say I'm talking crash, but I stand by it. But no more than a couple of weeks. Any more would be unhealthy. Dos that echo. Fuck that… What word would your friends in the past use for 'echo'?"

He had to think for a few seconds. "'Shit,'" he informed her.

"Fuck that shit," she swore, smiling afterwards, pleased with her clever way of adapting the old language. "I like that. *Fuck that shit*. It has a nice ring to it. Maybe I'll ask Father to resurrect the term and introduce it to more people. It would be digital, wouldn't it, to have a popular swear phrase credited to me?"

"Digital *plus*," he said drily.

"Do you know any other good ones?" she asked.

"Dozens."

"Share them with me, Cassique."

"Well..." He hesitated.

"Go on. Just one more. Please?"

"OK." He thought for a moment and cleared his throat.

"A digital one," she said.

"It is," he assured her, then grunted, "Bollocks."

"Ball...?" she repeated uncertainly.

"No. Bollocks. Boll. Ocks."

"Bollocks," she said, trying it out. "Yes, it's quite a filling word. What does it mean?"

"It was a term that people used for testicles."

"Oh." Her face fell. "That's not really a swear word then."

"It was in the past," he said. "References to genitalia were some of the crudest words our ancestors could imagine."

"How strange. Bollocks. Fuck that shit." She laughed and clapped with delight. "What silly people they were, letting words assume so much power. As if a word ever really meant anything."

"Some words did," he said. "Some words meant a lot. And not just the taboo words. They had powerful digital words too, which shaped societies and minds and generations."

"Like what?"

"Like... *freedom*."

"Freedom?" Her face was a blank. "What does that mean?"

He shook his head and grinned self-consciously. "No, bad choice. Forget it. I'd have to take you back there to make you understand. It's not a relevant word any longer. So, tell me about the new realities that you're playing. What's so digital about them?"

Nijin began babbling on about how real they seemed, how Father had introduced new smells, sounds, and colours, and how he was channelling the adrenalin flow like never before. She went on to describe how sex in the spas was more uplifting than ever, how many orgasms she'd had recently, and...

Cassique listened and nodded politely when required, but he wasn't genuinely interested in her journeys and experiences in the realities. He was thinking more about that word he'd brought up, the concept of *freedom*, which was no longer a part of the world, no longer applied, could not even be understood by anyone who hadn't travelled back into the past. He was wondering, if freedom no longer existed as a concept, did that mean the people of the present weren't really free? And if they weren't free, what, by the past's terms, were they?

Unbidden, another word entered his thoughts, a short, nasty one, just as alien to the present world as the other, only in this case thankfully so. It was a word which humans had outgrown a long time ago. A word which supposedly could never apply again, not now that Father was running things and everyone was truly equal. A word he'd never thought of in this context before, which was beginning to trouble him mightily now that he had.

That word was *slaves*.

Curieshire.
No humans parented children in the present. Father personally handled that messy reproductive business, taking eggs and sperm from clients in the sex spas, using them as he saw fit. He bred

schools of children in giant nurseries all over the globe, regulating the number of births each year in order to compensate for those who had died, to keep the population numbers constant. Sometimes, when events demanded it, he'd breed extra numbers for special duties. For the past hundred and seventy-three years that had meant mostly breeding Fixers, since that was the area where human agents were currently most necessary.

While biological parents no longer existed, brief foster parenting was a popular hobby among certain couples. Father was usually happy to loan out one of his children for a few days, or even weeks in extraordinary cases. He liked humans to experiment with parenting, to give them an understanding of how awkward and time-consuming it was. You had to take classes beforehand, and there were a lot of rules you were obliged to follow, but most determined people who applied were approved for the process and allowed to proceed with the fleeting adoptions.

Cassique had wanted to act as a parent for many years before he hooked up with Nijin, but the opportunity hadn't arisen, since he'd been without a partner, and Father almost never farmed out his little ones to lone humans. Nijin had been less than enthusiastic, but Cassique had talked her into considering it, and when Father in a counselling session had suggested it might be beneficial for her, she'd agreed to a trial run at once.

It had been a fun day, looking around several of the baby farms, choosing a child. Father sometimes made the choice, and always reserved the final say in the matter, but you were usually permitted to pick one yourself if you'd scored high enough on the tests.

They'd debated whether to go for a girl, a boy, or a non-binary child. Cassique was open on the subject, but Nijin pushed for a male. She didn't come right out and say it, but he felt she was uncomfortable with the idea of having another female in the house, and most of her friends who'd parented had chosen non-binary children – Father had for a long time been breeding more of those than boys or girls, and they now outnumbered men and women – so he guessed she wanted to be different.

In the end they'd settled on Zune, a boy approaching his ninth birthday. There was no tangible difference between him and any of the other boys, but Cassique thought he recognised something of himself in the child's eyes (albeit while fully aware that it was a ridiculous notion) and Nijin was content to go along with his choice.

Zune, like all children of the present, was reasonably polite but not overly respectful. Adulthood started at the age of fourteen, when the young were sent from their nurseries to begin their lives as fully developed members of society, to play in the realities and visit the sex spas and provide a human presence on all the major technical operations. (A concession to the times when humans still believed they were masters of the super-computer they had built, and demanded positions be created whereby they could keep an eye on its activities.) No children lived in awe of their elders. They knew Father was the only real superior being on Earth, so they treated older humans the same as members of their own age group.

Zune hadn't especially wanted to go with the couple and had ignored most of Cassique's clumsy but friendly attempts to converse and interact during their time together. Still, he must have enjoyed himself on some level, because although a child always had the right to refuse to be adopted, he didn't object when they requested further parenting dates with him.

Cassique had relished having the boy around, despite them managing to build only a shallow, distant relationship. He took him round the world on the monorail, visited the reclaimed deserts, taught him how to build a snowman up in the frosty Alps (which had been re-layered with snow in the twenty-fifth century, after Father had got a grip on global warming and reversed what had up until then been a world-worrying downward trend). He'd been keen to demonstrate that there was more to life than the sex spas and realities, an almost heretical notion in the current day and age but permitted by Father so long as one didn't take the fancy too far.

Zune went along with the ride, but rarely bothered to conceal his boredom. This real world of Cassique's was a dull place compared to the worlds of the realities. Why waste time building a snowman when, once hooked up to Father, you could project yourself into a sphere where you were the one controlling every flake of snow, where you could be the blizzards in the upper atmosphere, the glaciers in the Ice Age, the cold devourer of some imaginary alien planet? The real world, he'd concluded – as had pretty much every human of the present – simply couldn't compete with the virtual realities, and only a fool would choose the former over the latter.

The only times Zune took a real interest in anything Cassique said was when he talked about his travels to the past, the Time Hole, and the strange Personal Time each Fixer had to learn to deal with when moving between the worlds of the present and the past. Those subjects fascinated the boy, as Cassique had known they would. Father could be an all-comprehensive teacher when he wished, but he chose to be secretive most of the time. Information in this world was issued strictly on a need-to-know basis. If you weren't a Fixer, you couldn't access the data banks and learn about their missions to the past. Everybody knew about the Time Hole, but only the Fixers knew anything technical about it. The corrupted past was common knowledge, but only the Fixers understood how deep that corruption ran, and how hard it was to bring the existing pasts into alignment with the original past, and what the consequences would be if the Time Hole collapsed and it turned out they'd failed to correct even a single alternate timeline.

He hadn't told Zune everything that he knew – there would have been severe repercussions if he had – but he was able to elaborate on what the boy had learned in school and enjoyed seeing the light in his eyes as he listened to tales of people long since dead and gone, and the tricky steps necessary to manipulate those who'd strayed from the path of true history.

They'd played parents to Zune for seventeen days in total. None of their close friends or associates knew anyone who had kept a child that long, and it was a hot conversation piece whenever they chatted with them in the realities or sex spas. They'd achieved a small measure of mild infamy, easily won in a time where an eccentric was a person who stirred their cocktails in an anti-clockwise direction.

Cassique would have liked to go on further trips with Zune and Nijin, but both the boy and woman had grown tired of the experiment. In the end Nijin was the first to call time on their arrangement, after a trip to the southern cape of Africa, which had left both her and Zune yawning. She wanted to return to her realities, without having to make any allowances for a child. He hadn't taken up much of her time, but she'd started to resent the few hours she was being forced to devote to him. Once he was gone, she could concentrate wholly on herself again, without having to worry about asking Zune what he'd like for breakfast or dinner, and then having to pass that information on to Father, so that he could prepare and deliver the food.

Cassique had seen Zune off to the nursery after their final outing, insisting on coming in the car with him, and had felt a strange sense of loss when the boy was gone, even though he knew it was silly to think that way. He'd called to see him twice in the months following, but Zune hadn't appreciated the visits and had made his feelings clear. Then the partnership with Nijin came to its natural end – Father told them they should separate, and both were relieved – and Father sent him back on several long, arduous missions, and the months turned into years (for him). But he hadn't forgotten about the boy, and the feelings his brief bout of parenting had left him with. Now that he was back in the present, and could think of nothing better to do, he decided to give their relationship another shot.

Zune was stunned to see him. He was in the middle of a reality session when Cassique dropped in on him, having served no prior notice, and resented having to break away from the fun and games. "What do you want?" he snapped.

"I just called to see how you are," Cassique said awkwardly.

"I'm fine," Zune responded gruffly. "Father looks after me, like he looks after everybody else. Was that all you wanted?"

The boy wasn't much older than when Cassique had last seen

him. He was a bit taller and stouter, but Cassique had been expecting vast changes. It had slipped his mind that, while it had been seven years or so for him, less than a year had passed in Present Time.

Cassique shook his head and forced a smile. "No," he said. "I was wondering... Well, would you like to spend some time with me? I'm on leave, and I've got loads of credit to spend. We could –"

"You want to adopt me again?" Zune asked sharply. "That's impossible. Father wouldn't allow it — no child has ever been loaned out for adoption a second time. Not that I'd want to be taken away again in any case."

"Not adopt," Cassique said swiftly. "I know that's out of the question. Father's terminals, I'm not a complete crash-head! I'm not suggesting that at all. I just thought we could spend a few days together, as friends. See more of the world, go to some areas we didn't make it to with Nijin, act like explorers of old."

"Boring," Zune snapped. "I saw enough of the real world with you. Dull place. Oily mountains and rivers and deserts and lakes. Default on that!"

"Well, maybe we could visit a few realities," Cassique tried. "As a team. It's been a while since I went on any virtual adventures. Maybe you could introduce me to your favourite games. I'm open to any kind of experience. I just thought it would be nice if we spent some time together, for... old time's sake?"

He finished meekly and looked away. He knew he was sounding like a fool, like something straight out of the twentieth century, but he couldn't help himself. He was suffering from a disease which Father had for once failed to diagnose, a malady which was about to change his entire life. It could have been easily fixed if someone had noticed, and he could have resumed living as before with not so much as a scar to show for it, but everyone in this amazing world was too busy pleasing themselves to take note of other people's predicaments, and so he was doomed by indifference and neglect.

The disease, which had wrecked so many lives in the past, probably more than all the other illnesses and plagues lumped together, was that giant, ruthless killer of heart, spirit, and mind — loneliness.

"Are you feeling alright?" Zune asked brusquely. "You sound scrambled. You haven't touched any of those drugs you were telling me about, have you? The non-prescribed ones they used to experiment with in the past?"

"No," Cassique said. "I just have all this free time on my hands, and... Say, how would you like to visit a zoo?"

"A what?" Zune blinked.

"A zoo."

"I'm not cognizant of that word," Zune confessed. "Please explain."

"In the past, when there were animals on Earth... You know what animals are, don't you?" Cassique checked.

"I know them from the realities," Zune confirmed. "And I've heard rumours that once such creatures were present in the real world as well."

"It's true," Cassique said. "There were more animals than humans once, some much bigger than us, some only the size of dust motes, all over the place."

"Where did they live?" Zune asked, curious despite himself.

"Everywhere," Cassique said. "In every country, the barren wilds, the built-up cities, up in the air, down in the seas and lakes. Many humans even let them live in their homes."

"Oh, come on!" Zune's face crumpled disbelievingly.

"It's true," Cassique protested, desperate not to lose the boy's attention now that he had it. "Some of the animals were unwelcome lodgers, like rodents and insects, but others were kept as... as..." He tried to think of the word. "*Pits!*"

"Pits?" Zune echoed.

"Yes," Cassique beamed, delighted to have recalled the word (and with no idea that he'd got one of the letters wrong). "They'd keep some of the tamer animals, feed and wash and play with them. They called them pits."

"And these *pits*," Zune said. "They have something to do with this zoo you were speaking of?"

"Well, no," Cassique said. "Zoos housed exotic animals, tigers and lions and elephants, rare creatures which most people would never otherwise have seen. The staff captured these animals in the wild, caged and bred them, and kept them in huge complexes known as zoos, behind bars, so people could come and see them."

"And what did they do then?" Zune wanted to know. "After they'd looked at the animals?"

"Well, they... took photographs, and bought stuffed toys of the animals, and then... went back home."

"That's it?" Zune snorted and Cassique suddenly felt very small. "They came, stared, and went home? You'd give up time in the realities for *that*?"

"It was fun," Cassique insisted. "People enjoyed themselves. You might too if you tried."

"I doubt it," Zune said. "Anyway, there are no zoos today, and I can't very well go back to the past with you, can I?"

"Ah, but you're wrong," Cassique said. "There *is* a zoo. Just one. It's a small place, not at all like those of old, and it doesn't have any of the larger, wilder animals – they died out centuries ago – but it's interesting all the same, with cats and mice and a couple of dogs, even a snake and an old chicken. They're very proud of the chicken. It's the last of its kind, and there won't be any more after it, unless they clone a replacement.

"Come on, Zune, let me take you to visit it," Cassique pleaded. "You won't find it otherwise. While it's not off-limits to the general public, Father doesn't reveal its whereabouts to anyone except Fixers. It's meant for educational purposes, for Fixers who are going to be dealing with creature corrections when they go back in time. Come with me, Zune. You'll like it, I promise you."

"I don't know…" The boy scratched his chin and pondered the perplexing proposal. "I'm in a digital *plus* reality at the moment and I don't want to fall behind the others who entered the game around the same time as me."

"You can enjoy the realities whenever you want," Cassique said. "There's nothing special about those. Everybody visits the virtual worlds, but how many people can say they've seen a real live animal? How many of your friends can boast of *that*? You'll probably be the youngest person living today who's ever seen a chicken. Won't that be some story to tell the others when you're not plugged into the realities?"

Zune was certainly tempted, but the latest reality was *so* engaging… He thought it over some more, then in a rare spontaneous rush, decided to gamble on the unpredictability of the real world over the guarantee of the virtual. "OK, I'll come, but only for a couple of hours, and if it's not as interesting as you claim, I never want to hear from you again, alright?"

"Fair enough." An elated Cassique grinned at the boy. "You'll like this, Zune, I know you will. It's a real adventure, something the realities could never offer. We'll be like explorers setting off in the old days to discover new worlds and cultures. It'll be digital *plus*. Dos, it'll be *operative*!"

"Operative?" Zune laughed. "I doubt it. Still, I might as well have a look, just in case. Father?"

"Yes, Zune?" A hologram of Father's head extruded from one of the walls in the room where they were holding their meeting. Cassique jumped in his skin slightly. He'd forgotten about Father in all his excitement and would have walked out of there without authorisation if Zune hadn't summoned him.

"Cassique wants to take me to a zoo," Zune said.

"The zoo, Cassique?" Father sounded confused, but that was just an act which he occasionally put on — it wasn't possible for a computer of Father's calibre to ever be truly confused, even for a microsecond.

Cassique cleared his throat. "I thought it might be a valuable experience for the boy. He told me before that he wants to be a Fixer, if they're still around when he matures, and I guess I still feel like a bit of a parent towards him, so I wanted to give him a – as they used to say in the past – a head start, Father, in case he ends up on a creatures crew." He thought this was better than saying he wanted him out of the realities for a while, to broaden his horizons — that might have sounded like a criticism of

Father, which was the last thing Cassique wanted to do.

"This isn't the era for head starts," Father said. "Everyone today is equal, and under my guidance, all have equal opportunities when they come of age. Granting Zune an advantage over the others at this tender age wouldn't be fair. That sort of favouritism creates racism, sexism, war. You, of all people, having seen this in your trips to the past, should understand."

"Well, yes, I agree, obviously," Cassique apologised. "I should have discussed it with you first, but just this once, don't you think you could make a minor exception? It's not all that much of an advantage. I mean, most Fixers never visit the zoo or have anything to do with animals. Most aren't concerned with it at all. I certainly wasn't, and none of the Fixers I've met in the course of duty were either, except for the one who told me about the zoo, and I mentioned that to you when I asked to go there the first time, remember? Anyway, there won't be any Fixers when Zune comes of age, not if the collapsing of the Time Hole goes ahead as planned, so it's not that important really, is it?" He was sweating, despite the air conditioning, and knew his mouth was running away with him, but he couldn't stop himself.

There was silence for a moment, a purely theatrical gesture, since Father had surely already reached his decision. Then, with a wry fatherly sigh, he said, "Very well, you may escort Zune to the zoo if he is willing, but you're not to share the coordinates with him, and I'll be monitoring your conversation all the way there and back. Is that agreed?"

"Fine," Cassique said with much relief. "No problem."

Although Father was fully capable of recording every word ever spoken on the planet, he chose not to eavesdrop without giving notice, at least as far as anyone was aware. Again, it was a throwback to earlier times, when people valued such outdated concepts as privacy and secrecy, when there were aspects of their lives which they wished to hide from their colleagues and neighbours. Nobody thought in such antiquated ways any longer — indecent behaviour these days usually amounted to no more than being overly flippant in the use of Father's name.

"And be brief," Father concluded. "You may spend half an hour there, no more."

"As you say, Father," Cassique smiled. "Thank you."

"Thank you, Father," Zune added.

"Have fun, boys," Father said in his best Pop-of-the-year voice. "Don't get too close to the animals or they might poop on you!"

Then he fell silent, and the hologram faded. The pair exited without another word and stepped into the waiting car in which Cassique had arrived. Cassique had an almost overwhelming urge to reach over and hold Zune's hand but knew the consequences of such an unhygienic act would be dire indeed. So, to ensure he didn't betray himself, he put his palms together, wedged them between his knees and kept them there all the way to the zoo.

It wasn't, by the standards of the past, an impressive menagerie. Most kids' corners of olden zoos could boast a more varied and engaging selection. There were no goats to cuddle, no giddy young lambs, no guinea pigs, no rabbits. The creatures weren't trained to perform tricks. Most cages were sparsely decorated, and physical contact was out of the question.

Two miserable-looking dogs greeted them at the entrance,

one to either side of the gate. They were on short leashes and, when the humans passed, they barked and made feeble attempts to lunge at Cassique's legs.

This turned out to be the highlight of the tour.

The keeper, an elderly woman called Grende, escorted them around the tiny premises. There were no signs anywhere, no informative nuggets like you'd find in earlier centuries. Instead, Grende spoke a few words in monotone whenever they stopped at a cage.

"Our cat collection," she said. "We have three at the moment, one tom and two females. One of the females is expecting. It will be our first new feline batch in six years."

They moved on to the next display.

"A rat. Rats were hated throughout history, often unfairly. They spread disease and destroyed food and goods, but they weren't as much of a pest as people believed and were highly intelligent. Some humans kept them as pets, though this was not common."

Pets. That was the word Cassique had been thinking of earlier. He glanced at Zune, wondering if the boy had registered his mistake, but his eyes were vacant and Cassique doubted he was even listening to the woman.

"Our snake," she said. "The last surviving member of its family. Many snakes were venomous but this one is harmless."

It was a small, dowdy specimen. Cassique had seen much brighter, livelier ones in the past, longer and sleeker, which hissed and slithered around dangerously and sent shivers down his spine. This modest relation hardly moved and looked like a frayed piece of rope.

The next cage.

"Mice. Very similar to rats."

The next.

"Spiders. Lots of people had irrational fears of arachnids, for reasons we have never really understood. They were, in the vast majority of cases, harmless, and a vital part of the food chain. They should have been prized, not despised."

That was Grende's most poetic line. Cassique was fairly certain that she'd paired the words accidentally, not by design, as she didn't smile or give any sign that she was proud of the description.

The next cage.

"Ants. Tenacious workers."

The next cage.

"A cockroach. A hardy survivor. They were among the last to go in the great cleansing. In fact, some were still at large in the world a mere forty years ago. We think they've all been eradicated now, apart from the few we keep here, but you can never be absolutely sure with cockroaches."

There were more displays, but not many, and all were as dull and unstimulating as the others. The creatures and insects in the zoo were always kept sedated or under strict control. Escape was impossible, contamination of the outside world inconceivable. A couple of hundred years ago, Father had declared that the planet was not large enough for more than one species. Humanity had shared in the past, but no longer. Earth was to belong solely to the humans from this point on. In the great cleansing, every last creature had been eliminated, and replaced with robotic counterparts if they were a necessary part of the ecosystem.

"Any word on the future of the zoo?" Cassique asked.

"Not yet," Grende replied. Cassique had learned, during his previous visit, that plans were afoot to shut the zoo, as it had been deemed surplus to requirements. "But we're not expecting to be open much longer. Father has told us he'll need the space soon, for a new sex spa. In any event, when the Time Hole is terminated, there'll be no need for a zoo — it's only here for the benefit of the Fixers who have to deal with animals in the past. Once they are no more, it will be redundant. We've already started curtailing reproduction among the exhibits, phasing species out — the pregnant cat was an unplanned accident."

"That must leave you feeling sad," Cassique said.

Grende turned and studied him inquisitively for the first time. "Why should I be sad?" she asked. "They're just animals."

"Well, yes," he admitted, "but you've spent most of your working life here, and I thought you'd have grown to like them after so much time. I guessed you might be fond of them and would miss them once they're gone."

She shook her head. "I don't mind caring for the creatures, because it's my job and I'm proud to be of service to Father, but I'll be glad when it's shut down and I can spend more time in the realities. This is a waste of a life. The sooner it shuts the better, as far as I and the other keepers are concerned."

"Others?" Cassique asked. "You mean you don't work alone here?"

"Father, no! There are eleven of us at present. There used to be more, but we've started cutting back on humans as well as animals, now that the end is in sight. Whatever gave you the idea that one person could manage this alone? Father's terminals!

Any more than three hours here by myself and I'd be fit for permanent shutdown."

"Oh. Guess I was mistaken," Cassique said.

"You certainly were," Grende said, regarding him as if he might be mad.

"People really kept these things in their houses?" Zune asked, breaking his silence for the first time. "Touched and ate and slept with them?"

"The pet animals, yes," Grende said. "Many humans were extraordinarily fond of their pets in the past."

"They were lonely," Cassique explained. "It was in the time before Father and the realities. Many people wanted companions they could talk to and care for, and trust."

"Trust?" Zune frowned.

"Humans weren't as law-abiding then as they are now," Cassique said, granting Zune the benefit of his years of observation of past people, and the conclusions he had reached. "They were prone to telling lies and many thought nothing of betraying an associate's trust. Domesticated animals were more trustworthy than most men and women, which was why so many of our ancestors placed their faith in them."

Zune shook his head and snorted. "Crash-heads!" he swore. "I'm glad I wasn't alive then. I don't know how you endure it, spending so much time among the barbarians. Any person who could allow a filthy, infectious cat anywhere near them..." He shivered at the thought.

"Different times," Cassique said diplomatically. "Different points of view. Each generation looks back with scorn on those before and considers itself the finest there can be. The truth is time makes monkeys out of all humans, most probably ourselves included. I bet there'll be people five hundred years from now who'll look back and wonder how we lived the way we did, how we put up with such *primitive* conditions, which is how our world will doubtless appear to them. It's one of the irrefutable facts of progress."

"No," Zune disagreed. "We've covered this in school. Father teaches us that sweeping changes were common in previous generations, but that was before he took over. He's created an ideal world. There's no longer a need to progress as a species, because we've reached our peak. All are fed and clothed and homed. All are equal, with almost unlimited access to the realities and sex spas, even for the masses who don't have jobs. We have everything those in the past ever coveted or dreamed of. There'll be minor improvements here and there, I suppose, but there can be no real change, since Father is perfect, and you can't possibly improve on perfection."

"Maybe so," Cassique agreed, remembering that Father was listening. "Perhaps I'm confusing the trends of the past with those of the present and future."

"No perhaps about it," Zune said firmly.

"You're right." Cassique surrendered quickly and graciously, not wishing to have an argument and contradict Father's teachings while the computer was tuned in. He looked around. "Where's the chicken?" he asked.

"The chicken's dead," Grende told him. "It was old and ugly, so we put it down. It was depressing everyone who came to see it."

"Oh." For some inexplicable reason, Cassique felt a great emptiness blossom inside his chest. Chickens were gone forever from the face of the Earth, never to return. It should have meant nothing to him, shouldn't have touched his soul in the slightest, and he'd never in a million years have dreamt it would.

But for some unknown reason it did.

Zune and Cassique were silent for most of the ride home. There was nothing for them to say. Zune had been bored rigid by the whole affair, while Cassique found himself upset, not just by the demise of the chicken, but by the apathy shown by Zune and, especially, Grende. Was he the only human left who felt something was amiss in a world without animals? Was he being overly, ludicrously sentimental, or did the problem lie (as his darkest thoughts sometimes suggested) with all the others? Had humanity grown cold and cruel with time, to the point where they were no more compassionate nor emotionally involved with their world than the computers and machines they had built?

When they reached the nursery, as he was exiting the cab, Zune spoke. "Well," he said, "I trust that's the end of matters between us. You've shown me your *real world*, and your creatures, and mountains, and deserts. May I put them behind me now, for once and for all?"

"Yes," Cassique said, voice low.

"You won't call on me unannounced again?" Zune pressed.

"No."

"No more surprise visits or presents or days out?"

"I'll stay away from you," Cassique said tetchily.

"I think you should ask Father about joining the Gemini project," the boy said, and Cassique stared at him with shock. "You might be happier in the past, where you can visit your zoos and live in your real world all the time. You seem out of place here. Perhaps you should find some ancient historical figure you can replace. I'm sure Father —"

"Enough!" Cassique snapped. "Your pubic hairs haven't even started developing yet, you little prick, so how dare..." He stopped, took a deep breath, counted to five. "Sorry, I shouldn't have said that. Goodbye, Zune. Have a nice life."

He turned, left in a hurry, and never saw the boy again.

Zune watched him leave, a frown creasing his face. "What's a *little prick*?" he wondered aloud, then shrugged and ambled inside. Some ancient Earth phrase, no doubt. Cassique was always coming out with confusing old phrases like that. He thought about checking with Father but was eager to return to the reality he'd been playing before Cassique had interrupted him, so he picked up speed and forgot all about it.

THREE

Hawkingston.

The planet's atmosphere was dwindling rapidly. Every step of the way Cassique passed people gasping for breath, choking, trying to inhale lungfuls of oxygen which was no longer present. He had a tank of the precious gas strapped to his back and fourteen minutes' worth left. He quickened his pace, noting that some of the elderly and very young were already dead, tongues extruding from their mouths, black, thick, bloated.

Destroying the alien centre wasn't the final solution. At most it would buy the planet an extra couple of days, by which time a new station would doubtless be erected. But a lot could happen in two days. If Cassique could earn his people that much time, as little as it was, it would give them a chance. When all was said and done, that was the most anyone could ever hope to offer.

He'd been wary of the aliens from the start. He'd been one of the decriers, marching against their apparently benevolent intrusion, warning of the danger they might represent. He'd tried to make people listen. He and a few others had stood firm and resisted the impulse to embrace the seemingly saintly new arrivals and accept their advanced technology. He'd said they should learn more about the space creatures, should study and examine them. But no one had listened. They'd all thought the visitors were the best thing since the invention of crotchless trousers, and now here humanity floundered, the entire race mere minutes away from extinction.

It turned out the aliens wanted the planet for themselves. They roamed the galaxy, searching for developed worlds they could usurp and inhabit. They'd built the atmospheric detractor, which was supposed to be a transporter, and were even now in the final stages of sucking all of the oxygen out of the air, making life impossible for the planet's current inhabitants. They would incinerate the bodies later or ship them off to an empty corner of space, and then they'd simply move into the deserted buildings, take over the monorail system, and program Father to cater to their needs rather than humanity's.

Only one man could put a halt to their plans. Only one man could buy the world the time it needed to organise and mount a decent defence.

And he had less than twelve minutes left to do so.

Cassique was within sight of the complex. The aliens were nowhere to be seen. That was their soft point, their Achilles heel — they were overconfident. They saw no real threat from the humans and so, rather than stay and see the job through, they'd left their machines to keep the people back.

The lasers began firing without warning as soon as Cassique came within range. He dodged the first few blasts, rushing forward the extra metres he needed, then hit the button on his belt, activating the scrambling device.

The lasers fell dead.

Cassique sped towards the huge building, running faster than he ever had before, one eye on the plan of the interior on his tablet, the other on his falling oxygen indicator. It was going to be tight. One slip and he'd be too late.

He could hear the machines clicking overhead as he entered the cool alien construction. The scrambler would be overridden in six minutes tops. He wasn't sure if they could get him once he was inside, but if they could he wouldn't have to worry about the lack of oxygen, because he'd be dead long before his tank ran dry.

It was confusing inside. He'd studied the plans meticulously, but they hadn't really prepared him for the labyrinths and shifting levels, for the tunnels he had to crawl through, the walls he had to climb. He forced himself, against every instinct, to slow to a jog. There was no point racing if he got lost. Speed was important, but it would mean nothing if he wasn't accurate.

The place was dimly lit, and colder the further in he ventured. He began to wish he'd brought a groin cover, since his exposed genitalia were bearing the brunt of the cold, but it was too late for that now. Too late for everything except the one remaining course.

He heard the lasers above click into functioning mode again. He held his breath and sped up. It took them a few seconds to lock onto his movement, and then the area around his body was filled with shrieking blasts and explosions and sparks. He narrowed his eyes to slits and ran through the chaos. He took dozens of minor hits on his arms and legs, groin and head, but nothing that could slow or stop him.

It seemed an eternity, but it was only eleven seconds, and then he had made it. He burst through a thin glass door and was in the central control room, the heart of the building. There were no lasers here, not in so sensitive an area, and he was able to pause for the first time that long, arduous hour. He wiped the back of a hand across his forehead and grinned.

He'd made it!

As the realisation seeped in, he started to laugh. Against all the odds, when it seemed it was far too late to turn any table, he'd come through all the obstacles and proved humanity wasn't quite over and done with.

He sat on the floor and began unpacking the explosives which were wrapped around his waist. He'd brought as much as he could carry, more than enough to deal with the problem at hand. He stuck his explosive plasticine to every surface he could find, covering all sides of the room, making sure maximum devastation would be achieved.

When he'd finished, he stood back and checked his oxygen. Almost two minutes to spare. Dos, but he'd done well. If it wasn't for that setback early in the chase, when he'd been waylaid by that dark traitor Phid, he might even have had time to make a break for the outside again. Still, he'd known going in that escape would always be a bonus, an unlikelihood to be grabbed if it presented itself, but not one he could realistically hope for. *Suicide Mission* was what Father had said to him when he was setting out. He'd understood and accepted the assignment and had no trouble living – *dying* – with his decision now.

Ignoring the timers, Cassique linked all the explosives to the manual detonator. He paused with his hand on the switch, savoured one last drag of sweet, sweet oxygen, then blew the mother.

They saw the explosion from miles around, those struggling human survivors, and knew immediately what it meant. As oxygen returned to the atmosphere, and they were able to breathe once again, they cheered and shouted Cassique's name to the heavens, honouring the fallen hero who had died so that so many others might live.

They wouldn't forget him. So long as humans strode the face of this planet, the name of Cassique, and the legend attached to it, would be on every pair of lips. That was a promise Father and humanity would always keep.

The end.

Cassique unhooked the last of the electrodes and removed the warm olfactory plugs. His legs were heavy from all the running, but a shot of uppers soon had them back in full working order. He noticed, in one of the room's many mirrors, that Father had spent the hours of play grooming and styling him. His hair had been trimmed, his pubes were gelled and shining, his arms, legs, and chest were fresh expanses of waxed flesh. He admired himself, then began slipping into his clothes. He didn't think to thank Father — it was an expected part of life in the present. Father insisted on cleanliness and style at all times, and if you couldn't bother looking after such matters yourself, he was always sure to nip in and shape you up whenever he saw fit.

"Finished already, Cassique?" Father asked, his hologrammatic face appearing in the mirror.

"I think so," Cassique replied.

"Are you sure?" Father sounded concerned. "You've only been in the realities a few hours, and all the games you chose were relatively simple classics. Wouldn't you like to try some of the newest additions? They really are vast improvements on the older games."

"Not today, thanks, Father. Another time."

"Well, if you're sure..."

"I am."

"Very well." Father faked a sigh. "I hate to see so much credit go to waste. Very few citizens ever have the amount of credit to spend that you currently enjoy in your balance. You should start using it. It's doing you no good just sitting on account. You should be spending it on some of the digital *plus* realities that most humans can only dream about ever experiencing."

"I will use it," Cassique promised. "I've got loads of time left before my holiday's up. I bet, by the end of it, I'll have whittered away every last credit and possess nothing but fond memories of visits to all the top-rated realities in your system. I just don't want to overdo it too soon, that's all."

"As you wish."

The hologram faded and Cassique left the room.

Outside, on the street, he was less cheerful. He'd put on a pretence in the realities room. His even being there was nothing more than a show to keep Father off his back, to make it look like he was participating in society the same as everybody else. Cassique didn't want to be the sore thumb sticking out of the crowd, not in an age where amputation might very well be preferred to a simpler cure. He knew Father would deny it strenuously, but Cassique had his fears and doubts. He'd heard rumours – very discreet rumours, spread in whispers only among a select group of Fixers – that some of his colleagues had seemingly vanished from the face of the planet, and that if anyone asked after their whereabouts, Father would fob them off with a series of shady cover stories which were basically being used to discourage any searches for them. Nobody knew what those lost Fixers had done to earn the wrath of Father, or how he had dealt with them and where they might be now, but Cassique dared to imagine the worst, and was keen to ensure that *he* didn't get on Father's wrong side, for fear he would find out the truth the hard way.

The realities were a drain. Not so much on his body, which was fine after a few shots, but his mind. He didn't much enjoy the artificial worlds any longer, the way Father manipulated the senses to make you believe you were elsewhere, anywhere you wished. It was too easy. There was something inherently ignoble, he felt, in a machine which could let you live out pretty much any dream of your choosing, but only in your imagination, at the expense of the physical world. The realities were a versatile form of entertainment, exciting and exhilarating – he'd truly enjoyed his battles with alien intruders, at least while participating – but there was something wrong when it was all a planet's population had, when nearly all the people spent nearly all their time playing in a virtual dreamland, never doing anything for themselves. Never thinking, never improving, never evolving.

Father was suckling humanity. They had become a race of children, never really leaving the nursery, dependent on their supposed servant for every waking want.

These thoughts troubled Cassique almost more than the world itself did. He'd never questioned Father before, even inwardly, and knew no other person who had, not in any recent century. They were supposed to be free to think anything they liked, and pose any questions they wished, but Cassique wasn't sure how genuine that belief might prove to be if put to the test. He had a nasty feeling – though, admittedly, it was only a feeling, fuelled by those rumours about the missing Fixers, which could very well prove to be entirely unfounded – that Father's leniency was more the stuff of ambiguous legend than actual fact.

Cassique couldn't explain why his thoughts had turned. He'd been happy until recently, content to go through life and the realities like everybody else. He'd never found fault with Father in the past, never considered the possibility that humanity had gone astray and was being led further from the straight and narrow every day by the crooked computer they had chosen for their guide. He'd never looked back into the past and found himself envying the people there, with their violent, unpredictable lives. It disturbed him that he could change so suddenly, so completely, and half the time he believed the sickness lay not without but most certainly within. He should ask Father for help, while there was still time to put a halt to whatever disease had inflicted him. He was a son of Father, that couldn't be changed, and he should start acting like one again. Duty was never requested by Father but, after all he had done for humanity, any person slow to offer their all was less than a worm in Cassique's (occasional) view.

And yet, at other times he couldn't think that way at all. He'd look at the world, and Father, and think, *this isn't right*. He'd study the pasts they were constantly altering, consider the futures that might spring from them if time was left to run its course from one of those points, compare them with his own, and find the present greatly wanting in comparison. It was as simple and as complicated as that. He craved a world with more... Well, he didn't actually know *what* he wanted this new brave world to have. Just that there should be *more*.

He shook his head sadly and hailed a car. He had to do something about this treacherous mind of his. He knew people had suffered with their brains in the past, that many had been victims of warring personalities, but that needn't happen in the present. He could be cured if he only made his illness known — Father himself had told him he preferred to cure rather than punish, when Cassique had asked about masturbation. But he couldn't. It was part of the affliction, the inability to speak up against it once infected. They used to refer to it as a *Catch 22* situation in the old days. He could only hope Father would notice some erratic behaviour on his part and step in with a solution of his own accord.

"Where to, Cassique?" Father asked when no destination was forthcoming.

"Hmm?" Cassique hadn't even been fully aware of getting into the car. Now that his reverie had been disturbed, he found himself looking around the interior helplessly, not sure where on this planet he cared to go.

"Cassique?" Father asked again. "I'm waiting."

"Take me... go to... the Fixer station."

"Your own unit?"

"Yes."

"You're not due there for fifty-four more days."

"I know. I just want to visit. I'd like to see how the closure is going."

"I have all that information to hand," Father said helpfully.

"I'm sure you do," Cassique said, "but I'd like to go there anyway, if that's OK. I want to see Chert, if ze's not off on a mission. I was hoping ze could recommend a few new sex spas."

Father was silent a moment, executing one of his false pauses for reasons possibly even he couldn't truly explain. Then he said,

"Very well. Your dedication is to be admired. But please don't spend too long there. Chert *is* on a mission but should be back later today. Please don't take up too much of hir time. Like the rest of your colleagues, Chert has a lot on hir plate, and it wouldn't be fair to keep hir chatting all day."

"I'll be brief," he promised.

"Then onwards, merry human! Onwards till victory! Onwards till dawn!" Father sang – the chorus from a popular twenty-third century marching song – and the car picked up speed.

Cassique had to wait almost six hours for Chert to emerge. He passed the time catching up with recent fixings. They'd sorted Lincoln out once and for all, he noted. The Spanish Inquisition had been set back on track. They'd got a man to the moon before the end of the 1960s, as should have happened. The uprising by the wealthy elites against the lower classes in the twenty-second century had gone according to plan, and the countermovement in the twenty-third – in which every billionaire and most multi-millionaires had been hunted down and executed – was progressing nicely.

Flicking further through the reports, he idly noted that Rort had been successful in his Churchill incarnation and had followed everything correctly all the way to his dying day. Cassique hadn't expected anything less of him. Geminis rarely failed or had to be replaced. They were as flawless and steady as anything in the past could ever be.

He began to frown as he studied the latest facts and figures. "Father," he said, "is it my imagination or have we fallen behind schedule?"

"You are correct," Father replied swiftly, his hologrammatic face pushing up out of Cassique's tablet. "This unit has enjoyed an extended period of ninety-two percent success rates, but overall Fixer missions have fallen down to around the seventy percent mark."

"Seventy?" Cassique whistled worriedly. "That's very poor. We haven't been that low in, what, thirty Present Time years?"

"Thirty-three," Father confirmed. "However, such a dip was inevitable. It's disappointing, especially since we're so close to closure, but easily dealt with."

"Does this mean the closure's had to be set back?" Cassique asked.

"Affirmative. Assuming we can get success rates back to eighty-five percent across the board within the next six months – and I feel confident we will – the new closure date should be sometime early in 2857, certainly no later than the end of that year."

"An extra two or three years?" Cassique cursed under his breath. "Looks like the holidays were premature, Father," he joked.

"Negative," Father contradicted him. "The holidays could not have been more expertly timed, since every Fixer is soon going to be on treble shifts."

"*Treble* shifts?" Cassique pulled a face. "Don't you think that's a touch harsh on us?"

"I do," Father sympathised, "but it's necessary. The longer we leave the Time Hole, the greater the chance of a premature closure. I believe we are facing an almost certain collapse by 2866 at the very latest. We must work fast if we're to beat the deadline with time to spare. I would feel uncomfortable taking us down to the wire."

"I see. Does this mean our holidays are being cut short?" Cassique crossed his fingers — if anything could save him from the precarious future which he was beginning to fear lay ahead of him, it would surely be work.

"Negative," Father replied. "Holidays will proceed as scheduled."

"Oh. You're sure?"

"I'm sure."

"Oh."

Chert was glad to see him when ze finally came off-shift, but surprised. "What the dos are you doing here?" ze demanded to know. "Has there been a war out there? Have the sex spas shut? Has Father imploded?"

"I missed you," Cassique said with as straight a face as he could muster. "I think I'm in love with you. I want to flee into the past with you and get married. Will you have me?"

Chert laughed and slapped hir thigh. "Still the same old joker. Digital, digital." Ze removed the cover from hir groin and chest and breathed happily, relieved to be free. The prudishness of the past was a pain for pretty much every Fixer. "Dos, I hate having to cover up for the trips back. I don't know how men's sperm ever survived such conditions, and how women's vaginas didn't dry up and rot away. Underpants and trousers and skirts... such torture! I'm surprised humanity lasted as long as it did. So, what *are* you doing here, really?"

"I don't know." Cassique shifted awkwardly from one foot to another. "Can we talk? Do you have time?"

"I'm not sure. Hey, Father!"

"Yes, Chert?" Father said, appearing out of a panel to their left.

"How long till my next trip?"

"Seventy minutes Present Time."

"So that's, what, twenty minutes for the report, ten for the briefing for the next mission, five or ten to shower and get dressed, leaving me with about half an hour... Sure, come on through, we'll have a word in the lounge. I was going to have a quick romp in the station's sex spa, but that can wait."

They walked through to the lounge, a large relaxation area which also served as a halfway house between the present and the past. It was full of ancient bric-a-brac — pool tables, early arcade games, old-style sofas, vending machines, massive television sets, books and magazines. It was designed to get Fixers in the right frame of mind for their trips back and keep them in that frame of mind while they were dawdling between missions. It could also serve as a provisional holding pen for any Originals they brought forward into the present, in case there was a delay in transferring them to the correct facilities, as there sometimes was. Most Fixers skipped the lounge after a few years on the job — it was a dull place, fine for fresh-heads, but a drag for experienced veterans.

It was quiet, as it usually was. A couple of young Fixers were trying to play the original Space Invaders game but were struggling to make it from one level to the next. It was a universe removed from the games of the realities, where the body existed solely as an extension of the mind and could be as supple and responsive as one wished.

A handful of other Fixers were sampling old dishes,

accustoming themselves to the vile tastes and smells of the past, so they wouldn't look out of place if they had to eat in public. Others were sleeping, catching some shut-eye, a waste no seasoned Fixer would ever allow — there was ample time in the past for sleep, and only a crash-head wasted his free Present Time in such a way.

Cassique and Chert sat and watched highlights of some major sporting event from the past. "Is that hockey?" Chert asked.

"Soccer," Cassique corrected hir.

"And the ones in yellow," Chert tried again. "Chile?"

"Close. Brazil. That's Pelé, one of the greatest players ever."

"Soccer, hockey, Chile, Brazil." Chert snorted. "All the oily same to me. I don't know how you keep up with all those tiny details."

"It's not that hard," Cassique chuckled.

"I know it's not," Chert snorted. "I just don't know why you bother."

"All part of the job," Cassique said. "*Be alert, not inert.* One of the first things Father taught us, remember?"

"Ah, Father's full of oil," Chert grinned. Ze could get away with saying things like that because ze so obviously didn't believe hir words for an instant. Cassique wouldn't have dared mock Father that way, because he didn't trust Father as much as Chert did.

"I hear the Great Fix has been set back again," Cassique said.

Chert's expression darkened. "Don't talk to me about it," ze growled. "I heard about it a couple of months ago, Personal Time, and I've been synapsing ever since. Sometimes I think Father's doing this just to annoy us, that it's all some elaborate joke. First the Fix is set for 2848, then '53, then... Dos!"

"It's not Father's fault," Cassique said, defending Father as he was wont to do in most conversations of this nature. He and Chert often argued this way, Chert taking the role of disheartened sceptic, Cassique flying the flag for Father. It was rather ironic, he noted, given his current fragile state of mind, and allowed himself a brief inner smile. "Father's doing his best," he went on. "It's the Fixers who keep slotting things up. Did you hear what the success rates are down to? Seventy percent! I feel sorry for Father. It can't be easy, watching your best-laid plans go to wreck and ruin all on account of a bunch of useless crash-heads."

"Yeah, yeah." Chert yawned and switched channels on the TV. A pornographic show came on and ze watched with mild interest. "Hard to believe people used to get off on these things. How could they be so desperate? Mind you, I suppose it was better than actual bodily contact. I guess if someone put a gun to my head and forced me, I'd opt for the shows too."

"They had very dull pubic hair," Cassique commented. "Women in certain ages used to have some degree of primitive styling, with shaving and waxing, but men rarely bothered, and if they did, they usually only shaved it all off. I'd have thought, since looks mattered so much back then to a mating couple, that was an area where they'd have made advances more swiftly."

"Aw, their brains were so scrambled from diseases, they had a hard enough time telling one day of the week from another," Chert scoffed. "Any man who'd allow his penis any form of contact with another human being, or any woman who'd welcome someone else's fleshy appendage into her body... They were asking for it, weren't they? I'm just surprised RUSH took so long getting round to them. Things might have moved forward more smoothly on that front if there'd been more non-binary people before the twenty-first century. You beastly binaries were always rather limited in your thinking."

Cassique didn't argue the point, because he agreed with Chert. People of the past *had* allowed themselves to simply fall into the patterns demanded of them by the old-world genders. Sex had been a controlling, limiting, physical force, rather than the senses-opening, fantastical, virtual experience that it was in the twenty-ninth century.

"Anyway, we're not here to discuss the follies of the past, are we?" Chert said. "What's wrong? Why aren't you in the middle of your hottest sexual fantasy and pushing the boundaries of where you can go with your libido in the sex spas?"

"I..." He hesitated. Chert was the closest thing to a friend he had in this world, but he wouldn't have said they were especially close. They worked together, enjoyed each other's company, and shared a similar sense of humour, but as far as trust and kinship went... He'd have to be careful. "I'm having problems."

If Chert was surprised that Cassique had come to hir with a problem, ze masked it masterfully. "What sort?" ze simply asked.

"I... I feel... Look, I've been on holiday a week now, and I've got seven more weeks coming."

"Don't remind me," Chert groaned. "Lucky hacker!"

"That's the point," Cassique said miserably. "I don't *feel* lucky. I don't feel privileged or delighted or excited. It's been a boring week, looking for things to do, feeling like I'm on the moon. I spent a few days in a sex spa, and that was nice, but I'd had enough of it by that stage and I'm in no rush to book a return. I don't get much out of the realities — they're false, I can never buy into them one hundred percent. And... that's all there is. That's *all*! Look around the world, at all we've built and are meant to be so proud of. What's left to do with your life outside of the sex spas and realities? There are no physical sporting activities. No movies or books or nights out at the cinema or theatre. Nobody has hobbies, apart from a few fortunate souls with deep specialist concerns, but we never see any of those because they're always locked away somewhere, working hard on their latest project. I tried renewing contact with Nijin and Zune – he was a boy we used to parent when we were a couple – but neither wanted anything to do with me. They thought I was scrambled for even wanting to see them.

"What's there to do?" he pleaded. "What the dos exists in this world for someone who simply wants to idly pass away a few hours while on leave? What's there for *me*?"

Chert was silent a minute, considering Cassique's extraordinary outburst. When ze finally spoke, ze was atypically quiet, steady, compassionate. "You're not the first Fixer I've seen like this. It doesn't happen to many of us, but there's always one or two who catch it."

"Catch what?" Cassique gasped, not having truly expected to find any kind of an answer here. He'd merely felt the need to sound off and thought Chert would do nothing more than pat his back and mutter a half-hearted, 'There, there.'

"Whatever it is you've caught," Chert shrugged and Cassique deflated. "It's a disease or a virus or a blown brain fuse. There's no name for it as far as I'm aware. You've been travelling to the past so often, you've forgotten what you're going for, and grown isolated from the present. I don't know how badly you're affected — some can never come to terms with it, while others recover in a matter of days — but the fact that you're able to talk about it, and have acknowledged something's wrong, bodes well for you. I don't think you'll have too much difficulty kicking it. A couple of weeks, a bit of guiding help from Father, and you'll be back on your feet and raring to go."

"But what's wrong with me?" Cassique asked. "Why do I feel so out of place, so useless, so empty?"

"I've no idea," Chert said. "I'm no expert in these matters. All I know, from what I've seen, is that it involves scrambled perceptions. Some Fixers spend too much time in the past. They begin to think things were better back then. They start getting ideas about changes they could make, new worlds they could build. They see all the human contact there was, and how important people believed it was, and start thinking maybe their ancestors were right, that it's wrong to have a world where nobody touches anyone else, and sex is purely computer generated. They get the idea that being alone means they must be lonely, and that loneliness is the ugliest condition in the known universe. They feel like they have to combat that loneliness, no matter how extreme a method their sick brain concocts for them."

"I haven't gone that far," Cassique said softly, wondering if this might be the reason why some Fixers had allegedly been discreetly sidelined by Father in recent times. "I know how harmful physical contact can be, and I know loneliness was a dangerous folly of primitive people's meagre minds. I'm not a complete crash-head."

"I never said you were," Chert smiled. "I'm just telling you what I've seen manifest in some unfortunate others. To be honest, I kind of guessed this might happen to you."

Cassique was astonished. "You did?"

"Yep. It's usually the earnest types who come down with it. The ones who take their job a little too seriously, who study the past more than they need to, who are always looking to perform more effectively even when they're already doing a digital *plus* job. I'm not saying every efficient Fixer goes this way, but some do, and you looked to me like you might be one of them."

"Why didn't you mention this before?" Cassique sniffed.

"And highlight a problem that might not even present in you?" Chert shook hir head firmly. "It's no big deal. So long as you regularly remind yourself of the reality of the situation, and stop the rot before it spreads, you'll be fine. You're too resilient to let something like this undermine you. You'll bounce back, I'm certain you will. All you need is to focus and redouble your efforts. Force yourself to embrace the present, concentrate your energies on the here and the now, and you'll be back to your full mental peak in no time."

"You reckon?" Cassique asked meekly.

"I'd bet every last credit of mine on it," Chert boomed.

"I'm not so sure," Cassique whispered.

"*Try*," Chert said. "You'll see. You're stronger than the pull of the past. Give the sex spas and the realities a real go. Keep telling yourself that life is great in the present, that there's no hunger, disease, or want. There are no ghetto towns, no homeless mothers huddling in damp corners with their squealing children, begging for pennies. No hatred, no bigotry, no wars. It's the best time ever to be alive. You know that's true, deep inside, and I bet you won't have to dig all that deeply to realise it, once you start."

"I hope you're right," Cassique sighed, managing a weak, grateful smile. "But that still doesn't answer my primary question. What do I do with myself? I miss work. At least I feel like I have a purpose when I'm on a mission. My mind is fully occupied, and I have a reason to be alive. What can I latch onto while I'm waiting for my brain to heal? What can I do to keep myself ticking over for the next seven weeks?"

Chert mulled the matter over and chewed hir lip while ze was struggling with it. "You know," ze said after a full two minutes of heavy thinking, "I believe I have a solution. A tad unorthodox, but it just might work."

"What is it?" Cassique asked eagerly.

"Father might object," Chert warned. "I can't see why he would, but you can never be sure with Father. He sees angles the rest of us could never even imagine, the potential for troubled waters where we see only calm."

"I'll try anything," Cassique vowed.

"In that case, how about borrowing an Original?"

Cassique cocked his head uncertainly. "What?"

"You know what Originals are," Chert grinned. "The figures we extract from the past when we replace them with Geminis. The Abe Lincolns, Attila the Huns, Leonardo da Vincis, kings, scientists, and the rest. They're all stored away in the holding pens, right?"

"Right," Cassique said slowly, still not sure where Chert was going with this.

"Most of them stay in the holding pens for the rest of their lives," Chert went on. "Can't have them wandering around freely and causing problems, can we? But they don't *all* stay locked up, *all* the time. Some are loaned out occasionally, to Historians, to assist them with their studies."

"I've heard that happens," a baffled Cassique said, "but so what?"

"Why don't you request one for yourself?" Chert said. "You're not a Historian, which is why I said that maybe Father will object, but you could tell him you're interested in becoming one. After all, the Time Hole's on its way out, even if the delays mean we're stuck with it for a few years longer than planned. Every Fixer will be out of a job after that. Most of us will gratefully turn to the sex spas and realities full-time, but I'm sure there'll be a few who'll want to broaden their horizons, who'll feel a certain fondness for the time periods they've spent most of their adult lives traversing. Tell Father you're interested in developing a hobby. Ask for an Original while you're on holiday, so that you can consider the matter further in light of some first-hand experience."

"But what good would that do me?" Cassique frowned. "I don't want to become a Historian."

"You might one day," Chert said. "But even if you decide it's not for you, it'll give you something to focus on for the time being. From what I understand of the loans, you take an Original under your wing, bring them home with you, feed and care for them while you ask them questions and get to know them. It's a bit like adopting a child, which is something you said you enjoyed. It'll keep you busy. Plus, when you've spent a few weeks listening to them babble on about their petty lives and their ridiculous, out-of-date beliefs, you'll hopefully grow tired of the past and start to see how vibrant and preferable the present truly is."

Cassique considered the proposal. "It's dossing crazy," he said, "but you might be onto something. I've never spent much time with the Originals, just hustled them aboard a sky ship and packed them off for processing. It would be interesting to pull one or two aside, hear what they had to say, learn how they viewed the world. Father's terminals, I can't believe I never thought of it before."

"That's the problem with diseased brains," Chert smirked. "Can't see the screen for all the pixels."

"You really think Father would lend me one?" Cassique asked.

Chert shrugged. "I don't see why not. There must be hundreds of thousands of them – maybe more – tucked away in the pens, serving no real purpose. There aren't enough Historians to deal with more than a few hundred at any given time, I'd imagine. Hey, Father?"

"Yes, Chert?" The hologrammatic head materialised no quicker than usual, but Cassique jumped guiltily anyway, as if Father had caught him in a mutinous act.

"How many Historians are there in the world at the moment?" Chert asked.

"Six hundred and thirty-two," came the prompt reply.

"And how many Originals do they have out on loan?"

"Four hundred and eighteen," Father said.

"Thank you," Chert said, and the head disappeared. "See?" ze said to Cassique. "Why, you and I have brought back near enough that many by ourselves over the years. They're as plentiful and worthless as those early twenty-second century robots would be if we shipped armies of them forward into the present. He'll probably give you a dozen Originals if you want."

"One will do," Cassique said. "But who should I choose?"

"Does it matter?" Chert asked.

"There's no point borrowing someone I've no interest in," Cassique said.

"I didn't think you were interested in any of them," Chert laughed.

"I'm not really," Cassique said, "but at the same time I'd hate to draw a George Bush when I could have a George Washington, you know what I mean?"

"One George is much the same as any other," Chert yawned, then slapped a thigh again and stood. "Look, I'm no expert, it was merely a thought off the top of my head. I imagine there'll be limits, based on availability and safety measures — for instance, I can't imagine Father sanctioning the release of a deranged serial killer. But if he's open to the idea, I'd say there'll be a wide range of options. Cast your eye over them, try one out. If you don't like it, take the thing back and trade it for another. Dos, I'm starting to fancy the idea myself now that I think about it. I could interrogate one of Father's programmers and find out how to wrangle unlimited sex spa credit."

Cassique laughed and stood as well. "Trust you to go for the venal every time."

"Hey, it's how I roll," Chert winked. "Anyway, I've got to be scuttling. Reports wait for no Fixer. You feel better now?"

"Yes," Cassique said truthfully. "Thanks. You've got me out

of a real mess. I feel it in my bones. This is exactly what I need. A hobby. It'll get my mind out of the trench and, after a month or so, I'll probably be so sick of the past I'll go mad and hurl myself into the harshest, most testing realities."

"You do that," Chert said. "Let me know how everything goes, OK?"

"Sure thing. See you later. Have a safe mission."

"They're all safe," Chert sighed. "That's why they're so dull. Take care. And Cassique? Don't dos around with your mind. If the Originals fail to help lift you out of your hole, go to Father and ask him for help. Pride's a failing of the past, not the present."

"Wilko, captain, over and out," Cassique beamed.

"What?" Chert frowned.

"An old phrase. Heard it in a movie once."

"You're reciting movie lines now?" Chert groaned. "Father help us!"

"See you soon," Cassique smiled.

"Soon for you," Chert grimaced. "It'll probably be years or even decades in Personal Time for me. I'll look you up the next break I get. So long, Cassique."

"So long, Chert."

And then he was alone in the lounge with the rookies. He sat again and mulled over Chert's advice. An Original. A genuine, in the flesh Original. It was such a simple yet magnificent idea. Trust a non-binary to come up with it — they really *were* more inventive than the jaded old male and female genders. Maybe it was time Cassique asked Father to make a few tweaks to *his* body, to test if some key physical changes might result in some helpful changes to his brain...

Later that day, in the comfort of his own home, Cassique called for Father and explained about maybe taking up a hobby after the Great Fix, one that involved the use of Originals, and how he'd like to take an Original out for a test run while he had time on his hands.

Father was glad to see him take such an interest and proved more than amenable to the proposal. "We always need Historians," he said approvingly. "They help us better understand the many flaws of your ancestors, so that we can eradicate them from our flock as we move forward. We'll need them even more after the closure of the Time Hole, since they'll be our only links to the past from then on."

"Then it's OK if I jump the gun, so to speak, and borrow an Original while I'm on my holidays?" Cassique asked.

"Certainly," Father said. "There are limits, naturally. One general rule that I apply to all Historians who are just starting out is no people taken after the early twenty-third century — they'd know too much about the beginnings of our present age and might pose problems which a novice could struggle to cope with. Restrictions also apply to those with psychopathic tendencies, those given to suicidal fits, or those I feel could not cope mentally if let loose into the middle of our stunning modern world. There are other rules and guidelines, but you can learn more about those at the holding pen. Happy experimenting, Cassique."

And it was that easy.

FOUR

The holding pen was a huge, sterile complex where each corridor, with its array of cubicles on either side, looked exactly the same as all the others. The only people to be seen were the Holders, those responsible for escorting new arrivals to their cubicles and activating inmates for release to Historians. It was harshly lit, and although a moderate temperature was maintained across the site, Cassique shivered as if in a refrigerated room. He'd expected to be led to a reception area or meeting room but had simply been guided to a corridor where his contact was at work, and she dealt with him there.

"Who would you like to take out?" the Holder who'd been assigned to deal with Cassique asked. Hir name was Prin. Ze had gold-tinted breasts with luminescent nipples, and a lengthy, silver-streaked penis. Hir pubic hair had been grown extremely long, no doubt encouraged beyond its normal length by a course of glandular shots, and wound around hir legs in spirals down to hir calves. Ze looked bored, like most of the Holders that Cassique had seen. He'd heard that nobody ever applied for this job. Father lumped them with it and there was no way out until their time had been served. They racked up huge credits for their service, but he imagined that was considered scant compensation by the majority of the staff.

"I don't have a fixed Original in mind," Cassique told hir. "Could I have a look around?"

Prin tutted. "We house more than six thousand Originals here. It's going to involve a *lot* of looking if you want to check out every one of them. What's your field of expertise?"

"I haven't got one," Cassique mumbled apologetically.

Ze flashed him an uncertain glance. "But you're a Historian, aren't you?"

"No," Cassique said.

Prin looked positively uneasy now. "What are you then?"

"I'm a Fixer."

"What in Father's name is a Fixer doing here?" ze huffed. "I've seen plenty dropping off their catches, but I've never seen one come in to make a withdrawal. Does Father know about this?"

"Of course," Cassique said, offended that ze was questioning his right to be here, as if he'd have come without checking with Father first. "I'm thinking of maybe becoming a Historian when the Great Fix is over, and Father said I could spend some of my holiday time with an Original, to check if this is a road I'd like to explore more fully in the future."

Prin still wasn't convinced and called out for confirmation. "Father? Is this sap on the level?"

Father's head appeared out of a screen immediately. "He's digital *plus*, Prin. He has my permission."

"Very well." Ze tugged a strand of pubic hair into place and led the way. "So, where are we going?" ze asked. "We arrange these saps by era, year, nationality, and profession. You want scientists or actors, presidents or prophets? Egyptians, Romans, Britons, Russians? We specialise in post-twenty-first century Originals in this facility, but we've got a small selection of older specimens in stock too."

"Which are the most popular?" Cassique asked.

"The more recent ones," Prin said. "Mid-twenty-seventh century specimens are the hottest with Historians, but you need an awful lot of experience before Father will release one of those into your care."

"I can only go up to the early twenty-third century," Cassique said. "Anything digital *plus* from then?"

"Plenty," Prin said, "but again, we need to know what type. Do you want a twenty-first century feminist or a twenty-second century male equalist? A child or a pensioner, a politician or an artist? You must have *some* idea, surely."

Cassique licked his lips, which felt awfully dry all of a sudden. "I think... Are there any astronauts?"

Prin snorted. "Anyone who had anything to do with space travel is off-limits to all but a very select band of vastly experienced Historians."

"Then how about..." Cassique tried to think of a remarkable figure from the twenty-second century. "Verton Doales?"

"Operative choice," Prin said, smiling at him for the first time since he'd presented at the centre. "Unfortunately for you, ze's *too* popular — every Original we have of hir has already been booked out, and there's a long waiting list. Everybody wants to probe hir mind. The person more responsible than any other for the abolition of physical sex. You'd be waiting a *long* time for a session with a Verton Doales."

"In that case..." Cassique was starting to think this was a mistake and he should call time on it, but then he had an idea. "Do you have a spreadsheet I could look at, with the names and backgrounds of all your Originals?"

"Of course," Prin said and twitched hir fingers to bring up a projected tablet. "Will I ping it over to you?"

"I prefer to work on a physical screen," Cassique said. "Is there one around here that I could tap into?"

Prin scratched hir chin. "It's been a long time since I've used one of those. Let me think..." Ze looked around and got hir bearings, even though the corridor looked the same to Cassique as all the others he'd passed through. "Yes, just over there, if I'm not mistaken..."

Prin led him to a recessed screen in a nearby wall that looked as if it had never been touched. Ze tapped it to make sure it was working, then brought up the spreadsheet. "Father can provide you with details about availability, caring for them, and so on. Call me when you've chosen," ze said and moved away to get on with hir regular work.

Cassique spent a couple of hours staring at names and faces and reading their brief biographies. Most of the truly interesting Originals of that time were either out on loan or out of bounds to an amateur. He was beginning to think he should cast his line further back, to a less popular period, when one of the names caught his eye.

Beta D, a philosopher and computer programmer, had been a member of the team responsible for the development of the early realities and had pushed for them to work on a deeper, more spiritual level. He'd been airbrushed out of the history books to a large extent, and other members of the team were far more revered and better remembered, but Cassique recalled once chatting with a twenty-fifth century programmer, while on a mission in the past, who'd told him that Beta D was the real godfather of the realities, the human who'd truly *brought* the human to the virtual worlds.

Cassique studied the face and read through the profile. This version of Beta D was a mere seventeen years old. He'd been replaced when it became clear that he wasn't going to develop as quickly as he should have. Barely out of his childhood, he had never realised his potential as either a philosopher or a programmer, and wasn't faring much better in the present. He'd been on hold for eighty-nine Present Time years and hadn't been taken out once in all that time. It seemed that no Historian had any interest in a smart but underachieving kid, who wouldn't have gone on to become anyone of any kind of standing. He could see that there were older versions of Beta D too, and a few of those *had* been loaned out occasionally, but this was a virgin model.

"I'd like Beta D," he told Prin, who'd remained nearby. "The seventeen-year-old version."

Prin ambled across to check. "That one?" ze grunted with surprise. "He's never been taken out before. Why do you want *him*?"

"I just like the look of his face," Cassique said.

'*He looks a little like Zune*,' was what he didn't add.

"Well, if you're sure…" Prin said with faint disapproval.

"There's not a problem, is there?" Cassique asked.

"No, he'll be fine," ze sighed, "but you'll have to wait a few days. This being his first time out, we'll have to indoctrinate him. We can't send them out into the present all fresh and innocent, without any prior warning of what they're going to encounter. We'll activate him now, run him through the mill, feed him the usual information, prepare him for what he's going to encounter. Father will inform you when he's ready. I suppose the wait isn't such a bad thing in this instance, as it will give you time to learn how to interact with and care for an Original. I suggest you immerse yourself in the rules and advice over the next couple of days. It's not as straightforward as you might think. They need careful handling if they're to be of any use."

"I'll do that," Cassique smiled. "Thank you, Prin."

"My pleasure," Prin replied, then added with more resignation than bitterness, "Isn't that what I'm here for?"

Cassique helped Beta D unhook himself from the realities. It had been a long time since Cassique had seen behind the scenes of the virtual worlds which served as the true homes for most people in the twenty-ninth century. Father normally activated the visual implants before you entered one of the rooms, so you felt part of the reality even before you were fully hooked up. But Beta D had been keen to properly understand how the realities operated, so Cassique had escorted him into the room prior to the reality starting and was now helping him exit.

The room looked so tiny, given all the universes of realities that it could play host to. Four metres by four, and four metres high. In the early days, humans had been hooked up by wires and cables, and equipment like treadmills and climbing walls had been incorporated — the rooms had been *much* bigger then. These days, with the help of various implants, Father could mentally trick the senses most of the time, but he still employed a few physical tricks, such as air jets which could simulate acts like flying, falling, or swimming.

People still required food and water tubes, as well as tubes to dispose of bodily wastes. Many gamers spent weeks or even months in the realities — indeed, more and more almost never emerged, and spent most of their lives in the alternate worlds. It would get very messy very quickly without some old-school maintenance aids.

When Beta D had been fully unhooked, he staggered from the room in a daze. Cassique led him to a couch, where he sat and stared off into space, saying nothing for the longest time. Then, without looking at Cassique, he said in an incredulous croak, "*I* created this?"

"Not by yourself," Cassique smiled. "They'd been playing with virtual reality since the late twentieth century. It had advanced quite a lot by your time, but it still wasn't anything more than a novel form of distraction. You were one of the people responsible for developing it further, introducing smells, taste, and other stimuli. You actively campaigned to have it taken more seriously, demanding more funding from governments and big businesses, stressing how it could be used for medical purposes, scientific experiments and so on. The realities would have come to be without your input, as we've seen in various alternate timelines, but you were an important enough part of the process to merit a replacement when we started repairing the corrupted past."

Beta D looked down at his lap, then across at Cassique's. He was having trouble acclimatising to the nudity of the present. In his time, people had been taught from birth to cover up their sexual organs. It was hard to put the habits of a lifetime behind him in the space of just a couple of days.

"It's fantastic," he sighed, referring to the realities, not Cassique's currently flaccid penis. "I guessed something like this must be possible, and I remember arguing the point in school – that this was where the future lay, and we should be focusing more on the virtual than the physical, building our own new worlds instead of blasting off into space in search of them – but for it to have come this far, and to find out that I was centrally involved…"

"You were much older then," Cassique said. "You focused on philosophy in your twenties and didn't try to write your first realities programme until the age of thirty-two, and it was another six years before you began to really make progress as part of one of the pioneering teams."

"Thirty-two…" Beta D shook his head. He clearly found it an incomprehensible age. "I thought I'd be dead before thirty. The illegal virtual reality simulators – they were the only ones most kids could afford to use back then – were dangerous sons of bitches. They used to explode and fry brains on a regular basis. I knew the risks but went ahead anyway."

"Actually, you were seriously injured later on," Cassique said. "When you were twenty-eight. A model exploded while you were playing a game and you suffered severe cranial trauma. The entire left side of your face was hideously scarred, and you lost most of the sight in that eye. You spent several months in intensive care. It was only after that experience that you began to develop an interest in becoming a programmer. History views you nobly, as a man driven to protect others from the afflictions he had suffered, though we Fixers know you merely saw the opportunity of making big bucks and grabbed it."

"That sounds about right," Beta D grinned. He shook his head and stared at Cassique. It was a familiar stare, and Cassique knew the conversation was about to move on, to the thing that Beta D found even more astounding than the realities. "I still can't..." The teenager couldn't find the words and trailed off into silence, before yelling, "*Time travel!* Buddha on toast! I'd swear I was dreaming, or still in one of your realities, if it wasn't so fucking real. And you can go back to *any* time you want and pull people out of their timeline? From anywhere at all?"

"Back to around three thousand years BC, yes," Cassique said.

"But how?" Beta D asked. "And why the limit to that period? And doesn't it affect the future – your present – when you mess about with the past? And could *I* go back as well?"

He would have gone on asking questions, but a sympathetic Cassique raised a calming hand to stop him.

"I understand your confusion," Cassique said, "and I genuinely would like to explain how things work, but it's not permitted. We can only discuss these matters with a very few Originals, and you're not one of them. Sorry."

"Shit." Beta D stared at Cassique again. "And I've really been here eighty-nine years, asleep all that time?"

"In hibernation, yes," Cassique said. "We keep all of the Originals alive when we extract them and place them in hibernation chambers. This is a humanitarian society. We kill nobody, even if they've committed the most heinous of crimes in the past."

"And I'll be going back to that glorified *freezer* when you're through studying me?" Beta D asked unhappily.

"I'm afraid so," Cassique said.

"How long can they keep me alive in there?" Beta D asked.

Cassique shrugged. "Not indefinitely, but as near to it as makes little realistic difference. It's predicted that most people's bodies will start to break down after a few thousand years. If that proves to be the case, Father will free each of you as you hit that point, to live out the remainder of your life. Some will have to remain in confinement, if they're judged a risk to the world at large or if Father thinks they won't be able to adapt, but we expect most will be able to become full, free citizens, with all the rights and privileges that entails."

"Well, it's good to know I have something to look forward to, a few thousand years from now," Beta D snarled.

"I'm glad you see it that way," Cassique beamed.

"I was being sarcastic, you moron!" Beta D shouted.

"Oh," Cassique said, his face falling.

"Who do you assholes think you are?" The boy sprang to his feet and roved the room, waving his hands around wildly. Cassique watched in startled silence, mouth agape. "You come back, kidnap me because I'm not living up to some historical fucking standard that you insist on holding me to, stick me on ice for the better part of a century, thaw me out just so you can poke around inside my brain a bit, then tell me, as calmly as you like, that I'm going back to sleep as soon as you grow bored of me, but I *might* be released thousands of years from now, if my body starts falling to pieces. Fuck! Why don't you just euthanise us outright? It's not like we have anything to live for. You think this is any sort of a life for a person? How would you like it if some fucker from *your* future came back and whisked you away before you could live your life through in your own, natural time?"

"That's... That won't happen," Cassique said, shaken by Beta D's outburst. "Time travel will be abolished soon, and will never again —"

"Oh, it will, will it?" Beta D jeered. "How damned convenient.

Protecting your own asses, huh? Don't want your grandkids coming back to screw you like you've screwed us? Wise move. Very fucking wise."

"You're being unfairly hostile," Cassique complained. "If it wasn't for my intervention, you'd still be in hibernation."

"I'd fucking prefer it!" Beta D screamed. "When I was on ice, at least I didn't know how screwed I was. I didn't know my entire future had been whipped away from me."

Cassique bowed his head miserably. This wasn't going at all like he'd hoped or expected. Father had warned him that he might meet with some initial hostility, but nothing had prepared him for this.

"I can take you back now, if you like," he said meekly.

"Back?" Beta D blinked.

"To the holding pen," Cassique said.

"Are you threatening me?" Beta D asked suspiciously.

"No," Cassique frowned. "I'm just trying to help. If you feel aggrieved, and don't enjoy my company, I'll take you back. I'd hoped to host you for a few weeks at least, but it would be wrong of me to keep you against your will. I'll return you and try another Original. I apologise if I've upset you. I never meant to be insensitive. I'm new at this. Sorry."

"The fuck with sorry," Beta D huffed. "I'm staying with you. They're going to have to drag me kicking and screaming back to that place."

"But I thought you were angry," a confused Cassique bleated. "You seemed ever so resentful a few moments ago."

"I *resent* your people having whipped me out of my time," Beta D growled. "I resent your removing me from my home, my life, my friends. I resent your sticking me in a cooler for so long. I resent the fact that you speak so calmly of sending me back to a millennia-long coma. I can't comprehend how any decent human could do that to another. In a sick kind of way, you could argue it's worse than murder. But at the same time, being out here and conscious is better than slowly rotting away on ice. Please don't send me back. You've stolen one life from me already. Don't steal another."

"I haven't stolen anything." Cassique felt oddly uncomfortable. He'd never questioned the ethics of his job before. He was following Father's will, protecting the present. He'd never considered the fate of those he raided from the past. "You had to be replaced. You weren't functioning as you should. It's complicated, and I can't tell you much about it, but trust me, the entire fate of this present world depended on us taking you when we did. I know you find that hard to believe, but it's true."

Beta D scratched his left ear. "I thought you said I wasn't that important, just a valuable team member."

"That's right," Cassique said. "You're a tiny historical footnote, a miniscule player who'd most assuredly have been forgotten about if time travel had never become a thing. But since time travel *is* a thing, many small players have come to assume massive importance. You didn't change the world in a major way, but you left a mark and made an impact. Historically speaking, from our standpoint that makes you every bit the equal of Isaac Newton."

Beta D's jaw literally dropped. "Really?" he gasped.

"Really," Cassique said grimly.

"Who'd have thought it," Beta B wondered aloud, a little

smile dancing across his lips. "Me, the equal of Newton. Newton's my idol. Albert Einstein said he was the smartest person who ever existed, and who am I to argue with Einstein? To think they told me in school that I was on a hiding to nothing, wasting my time on dumb computer games. Hah!"

"So, you want to stay with me a while longer?" Cassique asked.

"Of course," Beta D grinned. "Hell, the longer the better. Maybe I can work out some way to escape and run away to another city or country. I'm sure I wouldn't be the first Original to slip the net, right? There's probably an underground organisation out there I can link up with, and they can help me start a whole new life, or return me to my original... what did you call it... timeline?"

"No." Cassique shook his head firmly. "You need to put those thoughts behind you."

"Sure," Beta D smirked. "I bet that's what all the captors say."

"No, I mean it," Cassique said earnestly. "Things have changed since your time. The world as you knew it no longer exists. There are no more countries, for one thing."

"Say what?" Beta D snorted dubiously.

"Countries are still there physically," Cassique said, "but there are no political or cultural divides anymore. They aren't even generally referred to by names — we only use names for cities, and they tend to be named after scientists, whose work impacted on – and thus can be claimed by – the entire globe. We're one world, united under a single banner. The United States of America, Russia, China, the African Nations, the European Union... those places no longer exist. They're just land clusters, geographical anomalies, nothing more. One Earth, one People. It's been that way a long time. There's no place for you to seek asylum, even if you could somehow evade Father, which you couldn't."

"You're shitting me," a crestfallen Beta D said.

"No," Cassique said.

"You mean it's all the same?" Beta D asked. "Everywhere you go?"

Cassique nodded. "Cultural identities were surrendered in favour of unification. Country names have been willingly forgotten, though some people — for instance, Fixers and Historians — do recall them. Colour, race and creed are all non-starters in today's world. There are no wars, no hunger, only one currency, which isn't in fact a currency at all, just a straightforward credits system which rewards good workers with better options in the realities and sex spas. All people are born completely equal and die as equals too. So, you see, there's no place for you to go. Father's monitors are everywhere. Father's children are everywhere. Hiding is impossible. Escape doesn't even exist as a concept in the present."

"Shit." Beta D covered his head with his hands and brooded silently and glumly for a couple of minutes. Eventually he looked up and asked, "But you'll keep me? You won't send me back?"

"I'll happily keep you as long as I can," Cassique replied, "but you'll have to return to the holding pens when my holiday runs out, in six weeks or so. They'll expect you back after that. I'm sorry."

"Six weeks." Beta D nodded submissively. "I don't know if it'll make up for a lost life and eighty-nine wasted years, but I'll have to make the most of it, right, and be thankful for what I've got?"

"You've certainly nothing to lose," Cassique said with a smile.

"Yeah," Beta D sighed. "Then again, there's not much for me to gain in six measly weeks, know what I mean? Still, no point complaining. Come on, man, let's go see this *one world* of yours. I was never much of a tourist, but I suppose, when in Rome and all that shit, right?"

"We're not where Rome used to stand," Cassique said.

Beta D laughed, his first genuine laugh since coming out of holding. "Oh boy, looks like you guys lost your sense of humour along with your country names. Come on, let's cruise a few joints, and I'll explain it to you on the way."

Through Beta D's eyes, Cassique saw his world afresh. As they sped from one side of the globe to another, the modern-day man began to appreciate the finer points of his society all over again. The way you were free to travel anywhere you wished. The elaborate monorail system that made public transport swifter and safer than it had ever been. The cleanliness, the order, the peace.

"Don't you have planes anymore?" Beta D asked at one point, gazing out of the window at a sky much bluer than his had been in the ecologically troubled times from which he'd been extracted.

"We have sky craft," Cassique said, "but rarely use them for everyday travel, as the monorail is more efficient. We use them primarily for our trips to the past, where travel is more of a burden, although we do also employ them on occasion in the present, to transport especially large weights from one area to another."

"You never invented a teleporter, then?" Beta D chuckled. "Like in those old sci-fi movies and TV shows?"

"No," Cassique said, grimacing gamely. "Research in that field continued for a long time, but Father ultimately dismissed it as an implausibility."

Beta D's eyebrows rose. "You mean time travel's a cinch in this Present Time of yours, but teleportation's impossible?" He laughed. "Strange world."

Cassique took him to the reclaimed deserts. Where scrubland once dominated vast stretches of the terrain, lush green paradises now flourished. The reclamation project had been humanity's greatest undertaking before the fixing of time became a necessity. The people of the world had spent more than a century, and most of their technical and mechanical resources, on the task. Few took any great pride in the accomplishment today – the deserts were taken for granted, like everything else – but Cassique had always enjoyed coming to the old wastelands and was pleased to note the admiration, even a touch of awe, in Beta D's expression.

"There was talk of doing this when I was a child," Beta D said, "but nobody seriously thought it could work, not anyone that I ever spoke with anyway."

"It became essential," Cassique told him. "The desert areas were expanding, getting out of control, and the issue was causing problems on a global level, affecting weather patterns everywhere. It wasn't that difficult once we'd started. Time consuming and gruelling, but relatively straightforward, like most seemingly Herculean tasks."

They visited the sex spas and more realities centres, where

up to five hundred people could interact in one game at the same time. They joined in a few, but Beta D, though already an avid gamer when he'd been taken, wasn't overly keen on exploring the infinite virtual worlds. Time was pressing, and he wanted to learn more about the physical world, not waste his weeks daydreaming. He'd like to come back to the realities later, he told Cassique, if he was ever taken out of the holding pens again, but he hungered to see as much as he could of this world first, to experience the future he'd previously only been able to imagine.

Cassique took him to visit the old Earth sites. Most of the cities and monuments of the past had been swept away over the course of the uncaring recent centuries. Respect for the past had gone out of fashion around the same time that crotch coverings had been dumped. The notion of preserving what you could of glorious, lost eras was one few people today could understand. The prevailing mood was, if it's old, it's useless. Still, scatterings of remains were to be found by those who could be bothered to look for them.

The tower housing Big Ben chimed as regularly as ever, even though the Palace of Westminster had long ago been reduced to rubble.

Lady Liberty's arm stretched forth over a land and people her makers could never have pictured, but New York Harbour was now dry land, and only a few low-level buildings stood on the ex-island of Manhattan, where skyscrapers had once risen in competing huddles to the heavens.

The Eiffel tower was no more, but the Louvre and its smiling madam were open for business. Beta D counted eleven people while he and Cassique were there, and you were allowed to touch the canvas of the Mona Lisa if you wished. (He didn't. It would have felt like sacrilege.)

Red Square had been preserved, as had the old Sydney Opera House. Two of the mighty pyramids which Cassique and Chert had so recently helped re-erect towered spectacularly in a carefully cultivated desert area (the sprawling city of Cairo no longer hunched around them to detract from the tourist experience), as solid and everlasting as their Ancient Egyptian architects had intended them to be. Several sections of the Great Wall of China still stood — most enjoyed next to no visitors, but one that had been converted into a sex spa saw a steady stream of traffic.

There were some other notable landmarks, but not many. Tourists from the past would almost certainly have sought a refund if they'd ever discovered a way to visit their future.

They spent a few days speeding from one tumbled-down, mostly deserted site to another. Beta D was patient at first, but gradually his interest waned. "This is nice and all," he told Cassique, "but I could see this stuff back in my own time, and a whole lot more along with it. I don't care about the past. It's the future – I mean, your present – that intrigues me. I want to see the world of today, how people live, where they work and how they spend their leisure time. I want to check out new buildings, new sports arenas, new monuments. What kind of music are teens into? Do you guys make movies? Is theatre still alive and limping? Where do families spend the weekend? I want to see how you *live*."

"Well, you've seen it," Cassique replied falteringly. "The realities and sex spas. That's about it, really. Of course, there are still people who work. I could take you to meet some of those, if you want to see what a current work environment is like."

"Oh, come on, there must be more to your world than that!" Beta D laughed, certain he was having his leg pulled. "What's the hot sport these days? Soccer? Hockey? Basketball? Something entirely new?"

"There, ah, aren't any more sports," Cassique said. "Not outside of the realities, that is."

"You're shitting me," Beta D hooted, but when Cassique said nothing, he saw this wasn't a wind-up. "You're on the level?" He whistled. "I was never much of a jock, but I liked watching the occasional game. Getting out, being part of a crowd, cheering on a team, gorging on awful fast food and drinking too many beers, even though I was too young to be legally drinking…

"What about the Olympics?" he pressed. "The soccer World Cup? Tennis? Horse racing? Swimming? *Tiddlywinks?* You must do something to get the adrenalin flowing. I mean, virtual reality is fine, but there's nothing like real human contact, is there?"

"I wouldn't know," Cassique admitted quietly. "I've never participated in a real contact sport."

"What about the arts, then?" Beta D tried. "Writing, painting, opera? Don't tell me the artists have all rolled over and surrendered to technology. That's something I'll never believe. Some things never change."

"All things, I'm afraid, inevitably do," Cassique contradicted him.

"No artists?" Beta D asked.

"I suppose you could say the last true art form was computer programming," Cassique said. "That ground to a halt about three hundred years ago, when Father's skills proved to be immeasurably greater than any human's. We couldn't compete with him any longer, so people stopped trying."

"You mean nobody creates?" Beta D was having a hard time getting his head around this. "Nobody puts their soul on the line, however ridiculous and puny their efforts might prove to be?"

"Not really," Cassique said. "Some Historians choose to recreate works of the past – the Mona Lisa, once-popular piano pieces, snippets of poetry – but nobody bothers with new work. It's pointless. All arts pale in comparison to the Father-generated realities. No book, film, painting or poem can match such experiences."

"Maybe so, but still…" Beta D rotated his shoulders uneasily as he tried to think of a pursuit that people of the present must still indulge in. "Singers? Surely people still like to sing."

"In the realities," Cassique said, "each person can have the purest voice that anyone could wish for. They can sing anything they like, immaculately, and always be wildly appreciated by a computer-generated audience. They can be pop stars, or rock legends, or folk singers, or opera divas. The realities offer perfection of a kind that plain old reality can't even approach."

"But surely –" Beta D cried.

"You must remember," Cassique interrupted, "*equality* is the key word today. Every person is equal in the realities, as great and wise and talented and successful as the next. Our entire society is based on that one great tenet. It's what humanity, in its noblest form, sought for as long as history has been recorded. Out here, in the physical world, that's impossible, no matter how carefully

Father controls the gene pools and education of the young. In the realities, it's a given. Like I say, the real world just can't compete. Why be a second-rate artist when you can be Pablo Picasso? Why struggle with words and come up short when you can perfectly ape William Shakespeare?"

Beta D hummed. "I see your point, but I'm not so sure I like it. I loved gaming, and occasionally prayed to a god I didn't believe in, to thank him for the invention of computers, as I wouldn't have wanted to live in a world without them. But to go to these extremes on the virtual front, to the point where your realities have replaced everything *real*..." He pulled up short as he recalled something. "What did you mean about controlling the gene pools?"

Cassique explained how Father selected eggs and sperm from participants in the sex spas, breeding children as he saw fit, rearing them in the nurseries where they were under his constant supervision. He told him the family unit had fallen by the wayside several generations past and gave him the usual, accepted spiel about Father knowing best.

"You mean parents don't exist?" Beta D asked.

"That's right."

"But what if you get a girl pregnant during normal sex? What does Father do then?"

Cassique frowned. "Normal sex?"

"Yeah, you know, when you fuck for real. I mean, you hardly spend *all* your sex time hooked up to a computer, do you?" He laughed at the crazy thought. "God, what an idea. Sex in the spas is fun, I'll grant you that, but it's hardly the same as the real thing. I must admit I'm not vastly experienced in that area, but

I've been around a couple of blocks all the same. There are some things a computer just can't copy, right?"

"In this world," Cassique said, "it *is* the real thing."

"Come again?" Beta D asked.

"Physical sex no longer exists," Cassique said.

Beta's D expression was a blank canvas. "Huh?"

"The sex spas provide the only outlet for sexual relief," Cassique went on. This was something he'd never had to explain before and was surprised by how awkward it was making him feel. "People no longer, as you say, fuck. There hasn't been a recorded case of physical sex between consenting humans for more than two hundred and fifty years."

"It's... You're... This is a joke, right?" Beta D wheezed, but when Cassique shook his head, the teenager's face wrinkled with revulsion. "You mean that mass of wires and circuits is all you've got? No more meeting up with people, laying on the charm, hoping to get lucky? You simply key in a few credits, hook yourself up, and let the computer do the rest?"

"Yes," Cassique said.

Beta D looked like he was about to collapse. "That's fucked, man. That's the sickest shit I've ever heard. How did you come to this? What sort of a lunatic fucking world is this?"

"Physical sex is... undesirable," Cassique said shakily.

"Undesirable!" Beta D's eyes narrowed. "You ever try it?"

"Father, no!" Cassique gasped.

"Then how do you know?" Beta D pounced.

Cassique flushed. "This a vastly different time to your own."

"Heh," Beta D said sourly. "Tell me about it."

"People think differently today," Cassique went on. "The values of your time, the beliefs... they no longer hold true. Having sex is a repulsive thought to us. We avoid bodily contact at all times. If we absolutely have to touch another person, we wear gloves. The idea of physical contact is abhorrent. For us it's the same as eating excrement would be for you. It's a taboo."

"By the eyes of the Prophet," Beta D croaked and rubbed his forehead with his fingers, trying to come to terms with a planet devoid of real sex. It was like some horrific sci-fi story, *1984* with jackboots on. "How did you get to this sad, sorry state? Was it Father?"

"It was common sense," Cassique said. "It began with a sexual disease called RUSH. It wiped out nearly sixty percent of the Earth's population in the space of two decades. Scientists couldn't find a cure. Avoiding it proved almost impossible — as it grew stronger over the years, it could be passed on by the least form of contact, a simple touch of a finger or gust of breath. In the end, when all looked lost, Father proposed celibacy and physical seclusion. He kitted out the willing survivors – some poor deluded fools refused to go along with him – in chemical suits and initiated computerised sex programmes. It was far more basic than it is now, merely a series of pleasing electrical currents and projected pornographic images, but it worked. Those who participated in the programme, lived. Those who didn't..." He sighed. "We lost eighty-two percent of our people to RUSH. Close contact was a mistake we'll never make again."

"But this RUSH is gone now, isn't it?" Beta D asked.

"Yes, but it could return if we lowered our guard," Cassique said. "And if not RUSH, then one of the other countless diseases that we've eradicated. Nature was cruel, so we had to find a way to best it. Our ways might appear strange to you, but you have to understand that every new generation strives to improve on those that went before. Each looks to eradicate more afflictions, and we found the best way to do that. We live in an illness-free world. No more flu, measles, cancer. We live longer than any people before, and more comfortably. No aches and pains, no cramps or infections, no dying of a degrading disease. It's Utopia, the dream of so many generations come true. If that means sacrificing bodily contact, eliminating all the animals, redrawing the sexual boundaries... so be it. Nothing's more important than life. As far as we're concerned, anything which threatens that life is an enemy and must be treated as such."

"I dunno, man," Beta D sniffed. "You think life's the main thing? I don't agree. I think *living's* the nub. Facing your enemies, fighting with them hand to hand. Sometimes you lose, and that's a bitch, but sometimes you win, and that's the biggest buzz there is. Forgetting your condom when you're in bed with a girl, the two of you deciding to make love anyway, breathing a sigh of relief a couple of months later when she's not pregnant and your dick's not falling off. Going to the edge, living with the danger, the uncertainty, the fear. Not everyone will make it, many will fall, but those who come through and live to tell the tale are the ones who know what life is truly about. They're the ones who've spent their time well and can die with no regrets."

Although he would become a respected philosopher later in life, at that young age Beta D had never thought of himself as a deep thinker or a great debater, but he couldn't stop, the words kept coming. "Your people are running away, man, burying your problems so deep you never have to even think about them. You might live longer than anyone else ever has, and you might be free of pain, and you might laugh at us *ignorant primitives*, but at the end of the day, what do you have to laugh about? You still die, don't you, eventually?"

Cassique nodded, amazed by the boy's passion.

"Death's the one enemy you can never beat," Beta D grunted. "And when you get to the end of the line, and the grim reaper turns up with his scythe and escorts you away like he's escorted everybody else who's ever existed, the time you've spent on this planet won't matter. The years you've got under your belt won't mean shit, because *eternity* lies on the far side of the veil, and a couple of decades here or there don't matter a fuck where eternity's concerned. All you'll be thinking about, as you set off on that final journey, is how you spent your time on Earth. It's the experience, man, the way we choose to live. That's what *living* is about. That's the meaning of the whole damn thing. The years mean nothing, and sex means nothing if you can't lie back afterwards and look with every last twist of pleasure in your system at the one you've just shared your everything with. It's the conflict, the struggle, that makes the decades worth shuffling through. Life itself is a joyless thing if it's served up straight, without all the messy, infuriating, wonderful trimmings."

Beta D fell silent, and Cassique considered the teenager's impassioned speech. He scratched his head. They didn't have philosophy in the twenty-ninth century. He knew nothing of the great thinkers of the past, their belief in the power of the spirit over all things material, their assertions that life was the tool and living the product. He knew almost nothing of hippies of the twentieth century and their on-off revival over the following centuries. So this was all a new sphere of reasoning to him, and it had set his thoughts spinning.

"How old are you, again?" Cassique finally croaked.

"Seventeen," Beta D reminded him. "Why?"

"You won't think so childishly when you're old enough to know better," he said shortly and weakly, and led the way home in a sullen, defeated huff.

A few days later, Beta D was thoroughly sick of the Present Time world, and his dark mood was starting to affect Cassique, who had taken to trying to hide from him in his own home. Most people in the twenty-ninth century chose to live in small apartments, not too bothered about the size of their homes as they spent so little time in them, preferring to chill out in the sex spas and realities. But there was never any housing crisis in this world, as population numbers were carefully controlled, so if you wanted to live in a mansion Father was happy to provide you with one, assuming you had enough credits.

Cassique's two-storey house hardly qualified as a mansion, but it was a lot bigger than most abodes, with two bedrooms, an office, a living room, a dining room, and a room that looked like a kitchen even though it wasn't functional — Father prepared all the (mostly synthetic) food and delivered it via discreet chutes in the walls, so kitchens had become redundant. It also boasted a couple of small, indeterminate rooms, where Cassique liked to store objects that he'd brought back from his trips to the past.

He'd left Beta D in one of those rooms, playing with an old gaming console from the early twenty-first century, and was relaxing in the dining room, sitting at its long, faux-wooden table, dreaming about being at a lavish dinner party and idly conversing with his guests as they nibbled on hors d'oeuvres. But it wasn't long before Beta D pushed into the room and interrupted with what was fast becoming a familiar refrain.

"It's dull, man," he complained, as he pulled out a chair and sat at the table. "This world is so damned *dull*. All you've got going for you are your realities and sex spas."

"I thought you liked the spas," Cassique said, trying not to snap.

Beta D rolled his eyes. "They'd be fun as an apéritif, but as the main course, the *only* course? Masturbation is just masturbation, no matter what sort of a virtual spin you put on it. Humanity's wallowing in an abyss of loneliness and the saddest thing is you guys know what you're missing – you must see it every time you go back into the past – but are choosing to believe that life is somehow better if you extract all that's truly human from the human race. I can't believe we've sunk so low as a people."

"*You* say we've sunk, but *we* say we've flown." Cassique shrugged. "This is the world we've built for ourselves, right or wrong, and there's no changing it now, so you might as well accept it."

"No room for argument?" Beta D challenged him.

"You can argue all you like, but it's futile," Cassique said. "Father runs the world and has done for a long time. He listens to us and reflects upon our wishes, but he's the one who makes the final decisions. Father has ruled that physical contact is dangerous and pretty much all of us agree with him. It might not stand the test of your ancient standards, but this is how the world is in the twenty-ninth century. If you want to be part of the Present Time, even if it's only for a few weeks, you need to learn to live with it."

"Uh-uh," Beta D said heatedly. "You might be prepared to lay down meekly and let Father steamroll you into the dirt, but I won't do that. This world of yours is an abomination. It's drab, lifeless, sterile. Humanity has rolled over and drowned in its own shit, and nothing you say will make me think otherwise."

"Be that as it may," Cassique said wearily, "you can't change the way we are, so why don't you just do your best to make the most of things and enjoy yourself? As I said, you've only got a few weeks, then it'll be back to the holding pen."

"Thanks for reminding me," Beta D pouted.

"I'm just trying to show you there's no point in wasting your time cursing and raving," Cassique said. "You're here. The present is what it is. Have fun while you can. Make hay while the... while the..."

"While the sun shines," Beta D completed the old saying for him, then pushed back from the table, stood, clamped his hands under his armpits and strode around the room. He reminded Cassique of the larger, wild animals he'd seen in old Earth zoos, caged in, desperate, lost. His heart went out to the boy, but his head told him that only acceptance of the facts could lift the young Original's heavy load.

"*You* understand what I'm feeling," Beta D said in the middle of his pacing. "You told me the reason you revived me was because there was nothing here of any real interest to you. You were bored."

"I wouldn't say I was *bored*," Cassique replied carefully. "I fancied a change, was all."

"A change to what?" Beta D halted and said nothing until Cassique reluctantly looked over at him. "What do you want from me, Cassique? Why did you bring me home with you? What did you think I could do for you?"

"I don't know," Cassique sighed. "I guess I wanted a friend, someone to talk with, who'd like to explore the real world with me, who knew how to make a life for himself outside of the realities and sex spas."

Beta D said nothing for a while. Then, softly, "So you want me to tell you how to live. You're sick of the realities and spas. You can see the truth, can't you? You know it's wrong, that this society that celebrates isolation is all some big mistake. It's going against everything human in us, and you want me to rescue you."

"Perhaps," Cassique said quietly. "I wouldn't put it quite that way, but…"

Beta D walked over to the older man and regarded him solemnly. "Sex," he said. "Find a woman who thinks the way you do, talk with her, discuss your lives and wants, your fears and hopes. Become her friend, and if you're lucky she'll end up taking you as her lover. That's where you should start. From there, I can't say, but that's the first step. That's where true happiness begins."

"I can't do that," Cassique said with alarm. "Father wouldn't allow it. Besides, where could I find a woman who thinks that way?"

"They have to exist," Beta D said.

Cassique shook his head. "No. Women today… men… the non-binary… They all see things the same way and think this world is a wonderful place. They can't *all* be wrong, so the problem has to be *me*. Inside my head, something has scrambled. I'm a misfit. You think I'm more human than the others, because I'm acting more like you. You think I'm the only normal guy here, but I'm not. This, the way I'm thinking and speaking, isn't normal. This is the voice of a man who's lost the run of his thoughts. I've escaped detection so far, maybe because my disease is in its infancy, or maybe because I've sense enough to keep my thoughts from Father. But nobody escapes forever. If there were once any kindred souls out there, people with similarly distorted minds, they've been captured and corrected. I could find no others like me, not if I looked for a hundred years, not in the Present Time. They're not here, or not walking around loose if they are."

"Then maybe," Beta D whispered, "you need to search in the past." Cassique stared at him wordlessly. "Go to the holding pens and look through their lists. Free a woman who might understand what you're feeling. Bring her here. Do everything you can to connect with her. Then, if things go well between you..." He arched a suggestive eyebrow.

"I couldn't," Cassique squeaked, flushing. "It would be... I might..." His own eyebrows began to lift, and an unfamiliar smile made his lips curl. "I *could*," he murmured, and the smile turned into a laugh. "I could!" he whooped joyfully and punched a fist into a hand with childlike glee. "I could! I could! I could!"

"You could not," said Father.

"No?" Cassique whimpered, dismayed.

"No," Father repeated firmly, with an atypical stern sting to his tone. "That is not acceptable. Gender presents us with no problems today, where all are equal, and many choose to transition through various forms over the course of their life. But, as you must know only too well based on what you've surely observed in the course of your missions, this wasn't always the case. People were often confused in the past, and confrontational. The line between men and women — and for the longest of times, those were the only two options available to humans — often resembled that of a war front. They argued and fought and dragged out the worst in each other. Those we've brought here from earlier times — except the most recent, who are off-limits to budding Historians such as yourself for different reasons — cannot help but lug those primitive mindsets with them.

"I have no hesitation in sanctioning platonic contact between members of the same gender," Father continued, "so long as neither party is homosexual, and I'd be perfectly fine with you choosing a woman to activate if your taste mainly ran to men or non-binaries, but I won't have you tempted and corrupted by the prejudices and conflicts of times long past. Male-female contact, where either or both is primarily heterosexual, is out of the question for virtually all Historians, even those with decades of experience. In a *very* few instances, where for some reason of research I feel it's inescapably merited, I will grant authorisation, but then only under my strictest supervision."

"Oh," Cassique croaked. "I wasn't aware of that. Sorry."

Father was silent a few moments, giving Cassique a chance to recover — Father was nothing if not considerate. Then, when he judged the moment right, he asked in what seemed to be a casual aside, "May I ask why you wanted a female?"

Cassique coughed and, to his astonishment, found himself

making up a story on the spot and actively lying to Father for the first time in his life. "Well, as you're all too aware, I've got an Original out on loan already, Beta D, and he's kind of lonely. He, um, wanted a bit of company. I didn't see any harm in that, and also, I thought it might be interesting to watch them together, to see how they interacted and related to one another."

"You wanted to watch them copulate?" Father asked with a chuckle.

"No!" Cassique's face dropped at the suggestion. "No, Father, that wasn't it at all."

"That wouldn't be an unnatural request," Father said calmly. "Many Historians are curious to study the mating behaviours of their more animalistic ancestors, and, given the correct, controlled circumstances, I often sanction such studies, but I hardly think you're at a stage where that would be advisable. It's a delicate matter, Cassique. The Originals have rather basic, instinctual drives, but they're not mere cattle. We must be sympathetic to their feelings."

"I didn't want them for sexual purposes," Cassique said again, reddening with embarrassment. "I just wanted to observe their interaction, how they speak, how they bounce ideas around, how they cooperate. I think Beta D is overwhelmed by our world and needs someone else to ground him. I thought a friend from his own time might help him adjust more easily."

Cassique could feel his stomach knot itself up from the lie. The cool Beta D, overwhelmed? Shy and reluctant to express himself? Crying at night, all alone, stranded in a time he couldn't understand, wishing he had someone from his own era to talk with? Cassique almost laughed out loud. He'd rarely met such an independent person as Beta D, one who could take everything in his stride, with a dismissive sneer and a thumb of the nose.

Father made a sound which was like a man scratching his scalp. "Well, if that's the case, why not pick another heterosexual male?" he asked. "Choose one before Beta D's own timeline, and around the same sort of age as himself, so he has to assume a position of responsibility. Then, as he explains both his own world and ours to the newcomer, he will surely flourish and grow. It's a method that has been used by many Historians to steady their Originals."

"Well, I... Yes, why not? In for a penny, in for a pound, eh, Father, as humans were once fond of saying. Do you have any suggestions? I wouldn't like to choose the wrong companion and make things even worse." Cassique figured he might as well get something out of this while he was here. Besides, he didn't fancy going back home to the brash Beta D all by himself. He felt like he needed an ally.

"Give me a moment." Father was silent for perhaps four whole seconds. "Ah! The perfect match. This is what I like about Historians — they throw up so many interesting, unlikely situations which I could never concoct by myself. I have just the Original for your Beta D. He's from an earlier time, so he'll have a lot to learn about Beta D's world, but unlike our young programming whizz, he's been out of holding several times before, so he'll be able to help Beta D acclimatise to our own era. Yes, it could be an intriguing match, a theoretical physicist mixing with a philosophical programmer. You'll have to keep me informed of how they get on, perhaps even allow me to sit in on a few sessions with you? Although our physicist has been loaned out before, he's always been rather tight-lipped, keeping his thoughts to himself, which has frustrated the Historians who hoped to learn from him. Perhaps this is the key we need to persuade him to lower his defences and allow us to get inside his head."

"Of course, Father," Cassique said, somewhat bewildered. "But who is he? What's his name? Is he someone famous? Someone I know?"

"Oh, I think you'll recognise his name," Father said. "In fact, if I may be allowed a small pun, I'm *relatively* certain you will. Go to the holding pen at the following co-ordinates. I'll have him ready and waiting for you upon arrival."

Beta D was sitting on the stairs in the hallway, nervously awaiting Cassique's return. He looked up eagerly when the front door slid open, and half rose to his feet but stopped when he saw a strange young man entering. Cassique slipped in behind him and the door slid closed again.

"Father wouldn't let me borrow a woman," Cassique said, "so I had to cancel that plan, but I managed to snag an alternate associate for us. Maybe three heads will be better than two, and we can think up something fun to do together?"

Beta D stared at Cassique, then at the new arrival. He smiled, descended the steps, crossed the room and held out his hand. "Beta D," he said. "Welcome to Shitsville, 2853."

The stranger, who couldn't be more than a few years Beta D's senior, blinked and frowned. "I recognise your reference to the year, even though it was 2847 the last time I was allowed out," he said softly, "but is *Shitsville* a genuine location?"

"Of course not," Beta D grinned. "These people are too po-faced to come up with anything so outrageous. Just my little joke." Then, when the newcomer said nothing further, he added, "And your name is?"

"Oh, pardon me," the man said with a polite little smile. "I'm Albert. Albert Einstein. At your service, sir."

FIVE

They nicknamed him Alb. It was Beta D's idea. He found 'Albert' too stuffy, while 'Al' didn't feel like a natural fit. *Alb* was amused by the teenager's linguistic struggles and willingly agreed to the new moniker, saying it was a matter of very little import to him.

He was twenty-four years old, hoisted from the year 1903, two years before he'd started setting the world of science alight with his brilliance. He was a moody young man, polite and courteous, but with a resentful glint in his eyes all the time. He said little and gave away even less. He was wary of Cassique, friendlier with Beta D, but suspicious of both men. It took the better part of a week for him to lighten up, to conclude that Beta D was a genuine kindred spirit, that Cassique really was a lost soul who was hoping to find solace in their company, and that Father wasn't working behind the scenes and using these men as pawns to trick him into sharing more than he was willing to share.

Alb was clearly very intelligent, but not obnoxiously so, and he came across as Beta D's equal, rather than his superior. Watching them together, as they discussed women and computers, history and life, Cassique wouldn't have thought that one would come to be so much more highly regarded by history than the other. Both were bright, alert, inquisitive. If he'd known neither of their stories and had been asked to pick the greater genius of the two, it would have been a blind guess.

He took Alb on the same tour of the planet as Beta D's. Like the former, Alb found it a disappointing experience. The Historians who'd taken him out before had kept him largely in the dark about the current state of the world, and he'd imagined something much grander. The social equilibrium provoked a grunt of approval, and the sanitation levels were certainly to his liking, but he found the technology curiously wanting. He'd imagined a more complex world, a quicker, keener human race. He'd been expecting gods, giants striding the world, in total control of their environment. Instead, he found hordes of disinterested good-for-nothings, spending most of their time gaming in the realities and living out their sexual fantasies in the sex spas, meekly following where their mentor, Father, led.

"How advanced is the space programme?" he asked one day.

Cassique blinked. "There is none."

Alb frowned and chewed his lower lip, a habit he'd picked up from Beta D. "But Beta D told me that humans made it to the moon in the 1960s, and to Mars in the twenty-first century."

"That's correct," Beta D replied before Cassique could. "We got even further than that with probes and robots."

"Robots?" Alb asked.

"Artificial humans," Cassique explained. "Well, that's what they were in the books and films of the twentieth century. In reality the *rocket robots* were fairly limited computing systems, built into the framework of the ships. They were able to control the rockets and take them places no human could ever go, to carry out various explorations and tests."

"I see," Alb said.

"But space travel had fizzled out by the mid twenty-fifth century," Cassique told him. "It cost too much, it was dangerous, and it was impractical. All they ever managed to do was send a few people up into space to spin around or walk on barren surfaces, and then bring them back here. There were no permanent lunar or Martian settlements, no city-sized space stations, no faster-than-the-speed-of-light craft or wormholes, none of that sci-fi jazz. The realities were the final nail in the coffin — with them we could genuinely go where no one had gone before and do anything we wanted in the worlds that Father created for us. They were cheaper, more exciting and less taxing than real space travel, and were open to everybody. Granted, they were nothing more than a virtual experience, but it was impossible to tell the difference while you were in game mode, and that proved to be enough for the vast majority of the human race."

"Humanity remains Earth-bound?" Alb sighed.

"So far, yes," Cassique said.

"Such a pity." Alb looked disconsolate. "I'd hoped we would have found a way to flee the nest, to extend life beyond the confines of so small a globe."

"Hey, you were largely responsible for shackling us to this planet," Beta D said, giving him a playful dig in the ribs. It unnerved Cassique to see the pair interacting so physically, but in their times such contact had been the natural order of things, so he tried to turn a blind eye to it. "$E=MC^2$ pretty much put paid to the idea that we could ever get very far even in our own solar system, never mind anywhere outside it."

Alb winced. "Yes, I've been told by previous Historians about some of my achievements in later life. But if my theories helped put the brakes on humanity's exploration of space, it almost makes me wish I'd been wrong." He flashed the two men a sheepish smile. "By the way, who was first to the moon? The Germans? Americans? British?"

"The Americans, of course," Beta D grinned, and Cassique recalled that the boy hailed from that long-disbanded country. "The Russkies nearly got there before us, but we finally brushed them aside and staked our bragging rights."

"*Russkies?* You mean, the Russians?" Alb's features wrinkled. "I would never have considered Russia a contender. Such a rural, backwards nation. Things must have changed immeasurably after my abduction. How peculiar."

"That's something I've been meaning to ask about," Beta D said, turning to Cassique. "I meant to bring it up before but kept forgetting. How come we can all understand each other?"

Cassique frowned. "What do you mean?"

"Well, I'm a Yank and I speak English, but Alb's a Kraut and he speaks German, and you… I don't know what language you speak, but I'm pretty sure it's nothing we had in either of our times. Yet we all understand each other perfectly. How come?"

"I still don't follow," Cassique said. "The English and German people spoke the same language as the rest of us, didn't they?"

"What are you talking about?" Beta D snorted. "They were completely separate languages, and only two out of many thousands."

"Separate?" Cassique shook his head, bewildered. "What do you mean? There is only one language. I know you gave it different names in your own times, but that was just colloquial, wasn't it? You could all understand each other, yes?"

"Of course we couldn't." Beta D stared at Cassique, not sure if this was some kind of elaborate joke.

"Then how did you communicate?" Beta D asked.

"They cannot understand the idea of different languages of

the past," Alb said quietly, interrupting, "because those languages no longer exist today. I learned of this from one of my previous captors. He'd heard rumours of a divided tongue in the past, a race of people who spoke in a way no others could understand. He asked if I could verify such an apparently far-fetched notion. I explained how every branch of humanity had developed its own verbal rules and forms, how almost every country boasted its own unique vocabulary. He was stunned. He'd never imagined such a planet, such a time. Together, with Father, we explored the development of global speech patterns.

"As all the old countries united into one uber-country, it was decided we needed a common language which excluded nobody. Father and the most learned linguists of the time took words and rules from every tongue and combined them all. The new language had no name, and it took some decades to fully catch on, but finally, with the abolition of the human family as you and I knew it, and the passing of parenthood to Father, all children were reared to exclusively speak the new language and grew up never knowing any other. In time they even forgot there had been such divisions."

"But how do *we* understand one another?" a startled Beta D asked. "We were never schooled in this new language. I don't know a word of anything other than good old English."

"Yes, how is this possible?" an equally flabbergasted Cassique wheezed, hardly able to believe that he was being taught such a thing by a child of the long-distant past. He'd always taken it for granted that everyone he'd met during the course of his missions had been speaking the same language as him.

"They have throat implants which distort their words and

convert them into our languages," Alb informed him. "They have similar aural implants which convert our languages into theirs. The implants are quite ingenious but can only translate their words into one language at a time, otherwise one translation would clash with another — if Cassique's words were translated into both English and German at the same time, we'd both have trouble making any sense of what he was saying. This is rarely an issue when they travel into the past, as their interactions with the locals are extremely limited, but would be a problem here for Historians who take out more than one Original at a time on loan. Thus, those of us in the holding pens all have them surgically inserted too, as soon as we're put on ice."

An alarmed-looking Beta D felt his throat carefully, probing with his nimble fingers. "I don't feel anything," he croaked.

"You can't," Alb said. "As far as I understand it, miniature computerised sheets coat our vocal cords all the way down to the lungs, while similar devices have been implanted in our aural canals, and they're impossible to detect without the relevant technology."

Beta D gulped a few times, experimentally. "I suppose they'd be handy for chatting up foreign exchange students back in the old days," he quipped, trying to make light of the situation.

Cassique, on the other hand, was still struggling with the concept. "You really spoke differently in the past?" he asked.

"There were similarities between some of the languages," Alb said. "Many were variations and alterations of other tongues, and they changed over time, but each had its own identity."

"And you couldn't understand each other if you didn't come from the same place?" Cassique pressed.

"It was possible to learn other languages," Alb said, "but few in my time did. It was awkward and rather expensive unless work happened to take you between different countries for extended spells, and global leisure travel was not yet the convenience that it became in later decades, from what I have been told. No doubt a citizen a hundred years after my time, from the early twenty-first century, would have been fluent in at least several different languages, given the ease with which they were able to move around the world."

"No wonder things were so dossed up," Cassique said, eyes widening as he mulled over this startling new information. "Father's terminals! Now I understand what all those wars were about. Not being able to communicate freely with one another... I'm surprised humanity survived such a mess at all."

"Oh, we managed to struggle along," Alb smiled. "Things were settling down by my time. Civilisation was working its way around the barriers of the past, such as language, religion, race. We have always been progressing and improving as we evolved."

"Hah!" Beta D snorted and treated Alb to a curiously sympathetic glance. "If you ask one of this century's Historians to tell you what happened a decade ahead of the time when you were taken, and another couple of decades on from that, I think you'll be in for a depressing, sobering shock, my friend." Then he clicked his heels together, put the index finger of his left hand over his upper lip, stuck his right hand up rigidly in the air, and gloomily barked, "*Sieg Heil!*"

As the days ticked by, Alb began politely pestering Cassique for information about time travel and the Time Hole. None of the

Historians he'd been with before had been able to explain the flexible state of time to him. They claimed they knew nothing about it, that it wasn't their field, and that they were as ignorant about the mechanics behind it as they were about those behind the realities.

"They were probably telling the truth," Cassique said. "Very few of us have any insight into the ways and means of the temporal situation. Father distributes such information only when necessary. Most Historians don't have access to that kind of data."

"But you do, as a Fixer?" Alb pressed.

"Well, I know what little Father has told me," Cassique said.

"Which is?" Alb murmured.

Cassique hesitated. "I shouldn't really tell you anything. Father doesn't like us revealing too much about the present and time travel. Some Originals are granted a certain amount of access to the facts, and I think you're probably one of the ones with more leeway than most, given your status as a key thinker in the field, but Beta D definitely can't be part of the discussion, and I can only reveal a limited amount."

"I see," Alb said, nodding sedately. "In that case, don't bother. I withdraw my request to know more."

"Oh good, I think that's for the best," Cassique beamed, pleased with the way he'd handled the matter. He left the house feeling rather smug and content with himself.

A few days later, arriving home earlier than intended after a trip to the sex spas – he wasn't *entirely* bored of them – he found Alb and Beta D in his office, fooling around with one of Father's physical terminals. Most houses didn't have such an object, but Cassique's fondness for ancient hardware had seen him track down a few hard drives and screens over the years, and Father had allowed him to hire an engineer to hook them up by wires to his network.

He frowned when he entered the office, craning his neck to see what they were up to, and noticed Beta D had also connected an ancient keyboard which Cassique had kept as a souvenir from one of his early visits to the past. The screen was touchscreen, but Alb seemed more at ease with something resembling a typewriter.

"What are you two doing?" Cassique asked suspiciously.

"We're studying my theory of relativity," Alb replied calmly. "I was quite the brainbox in my future, wasn't I?"

"Hey, you don't have access to that!" Cassique rushed across the room, at a loss to understand how they had got their hands on such restricted files. He saw that Beta D had opened the back of the hard drive and rewired it, and that was how they were bringing up files that should have been off-limits to a pair of Originals, apparently without Father being aware of the intrusion.

"How did you do this?" Cassique asked, dumbstruck. His first impulse was to rip the wires out, quickly – maybe Father *was* aware of this and was testing him, to find out how he'd react in such a situation – but his curiosity stayed his hand. He'd believed Father was immune to such old-fashioned cyber-attacks — he was aware of the ancient art of hacking but assumed it had died out centuries ago. The idea that a couple of humans could outsmart Father was heretical. Yet here they were, seemingly doing the impossible.

"Simple," an elated Beta D said, hitting a key to bring up a fresh page which Alb immediately pored over. "This Father of yours is too sure of himself. People today must be so ignorant of computing matters that he doesn't bother with proper safety measures, as he doesn't anticipate any direct lines of attack. Once I was wired up, I cracked his firewalls in a matter of hours, just a few days after arriving here, one night while you were sleeping. I have to be careful with what I access, especially if it relates to more recent centuries — stuff about time travel and the like — because a lot of that is more carefully protected and I'd almost certainly trigger an alarm if I tried to hack into it. But all the old stuff, everything from twenty-six hundred backwards, is pretty much out there in the open. Honestly, I was cracking harder codes than these when I was just eleven years old. He's slack, Cassique, slacker than any world-dominant computer has a right to be." He clicked his tongue reprovingly.

"We've been using it to inform ourselves," Alb said, speaking without looking away from the screen, nodding at Beta D for a fresh page. "We had a lot to catch up on, especially me." He shook his head and sighed. "We came so far, so swiftly. The twentieth century alone far surpassed anything I'd ever dreamt of. My God, even by the time I died it was in almost every aspect a different world to the one into which I'd been born. As for the centuries following..."

Alb laughed with giddy delight, then grew serious again. "But that all stopped with Father. The exploration, the investigations, the search for fresh challenges and new frontiers. He killed you as a species, stripped away all that was magical and mysterious, all that demanded the very best of the human race. He drained you of your thirst to overcome obstacles, your desire to explore fresh ground and improve with every new generational step.

"And what did he give you instead? *Games*." Alb spat out the word as if it was venom in his mouth. "He gave you dreams and visions and adrenalin stimulants. A fair swap? I think not. He's cheated humanity. Your supposedly marvellous, all-powerful computer has ripped out everything human from your race and built his own world of puppets and performing dogs."

"Well, you two are more responsible for that than us," Cassique whined. "You and your people built this world. We simply inherited it. There's no point blaming us for what it's become."

"I'm not blaming you," Alb said. "In truth I'm sorry for you. Never to know the thrill of the struggle, the yearning for more, the passions of love and hatred, the warmth of friendship and family..." He shook his head sadly. "This is a world of poor, lost souls."

"We don't need your sympathy," Cassique huffed. "You forget who's in charge. I can have you back in the holding pens in a matter of minutes. All I have to do is give the word and –"

"– Father will send a crack team straight along to punish us for pointing out what he's done to the world," Alb muttered. "Yes, Cassique, we know. But you're wrong. You might not want our sympathy, but you most certainly need it."

Cassique tried to hurl a stinging retort back at the young, twentieth century man, but could think of none. He stared instead at the flickering screen, then at the rapt faces of the two travellers from the past, then cast a worried glance around the room.

"Are you sure Father doesn't know you're doing this?" He spoke in a whisper, though he knew Father's aural sensors could, quite literally, locate a needle in a haystack if he was focused on it, simply by the sound of its shifting.

"Fairly sure," Beta D replied, though he looked worried as well. "It's possible he has a warning system in place which I didn't notice, and that he's monitoring us even as we speak, but I don't think so. As young as I was when you took me, I'd seen a lot of computers in my time, and while I'm not the expert I was by all accounts going to one day be, I know a thing or two. This doesn't look like an elaborate trap. It looks like carelessness on Father's part, an oversight based on contempt and disregard for a people who wouldn't even know where to start if they wanted to hack his system."

"Of course," Alb chipped in, "I suspect the best traps always look that way."

"True," Beta D grimaced.

"Dos!" Cassique sat and mopped his brow. "I'll be locked away forever for this or hooked up to the most terrifying reality imaginable. If he ever finds out..."

"What *would* happen to you?" Alb asked. "We've tried accessing the legal files, but they're too closely guarded. How would Father punish somebody who broke the law this way?"

Cassique scratched his head. "I don't know," he said. "Strictly speaking, there *are* no laws anymore, just Fatherly recommendations which we all obey because we've been raised to think it would be self-harming madness not to go along with them."

"No laws?" Alb frowned.

"No laws, no crime, no rules," Cassique said. "Father advises us on what we should and shouldn't do, and we comply. *Father knows best.* It's the first thing we're taught. We'd no more question one of his commands than... than..." He shrugged. "I can't explain it. I've seen the way your world works, the laws your people construed, the troubles you had adhering to them. This world is completely alien to that. The very concept of law has been altered irrevocably over the years. There are no restraints or legal boundaries, and thus no crimes or room for actual disobedience. If there are no laws to break, you can't really break them."

"But surely some things can't be tolerated," Alb said. "If a man murders, is he not punished?"

"People don't murder anymore," Cassique said. "Our brains are monitored and corrected throughout our youth to remove all traces of homicidal madness. Also, if you look at most murders from your time, you'll find the majority were related to sex or money. Here, we have no sex or money, so that deadly kindling has been eradicated."

"But there is right and wrong," Alb insisted. "What we are doing now is wrong, yes?"

"I think so," Cassique said uncertainly.

"You only *think* so?" Alb asked.

"Father wouldn't approve," Cassique said. "At least I assume he wouldn't. And, since we all try and live our lives the way Father wishes, I suppose, by your terms, yes, it's wrong."

"And Father punishes wrongdoers?" Alb asked.

"I don't know." Cassique covered his face with his hands and groaned. He was thinking about the rumours he'd heard, regarding missing Fixers. He felt that he should share those stories with Alb and Beta D, but he preferred not to repeat them, as he didn't want to accept that Father – the only parent he'd ever known – could be a devious enemy who eliminated anyone who got on the wrong side of him.

"I don't know what he does," Cassique said, lowering his

hands, and because he was lying to himself as well as to his guests, it didn't feel completely like a lie. "It's not like your time with papers, radio, television and – in Beta D's time anyway – websites listing all the details of crime and punishment. We don't hear about crime here. We don't know the laws, if there are any. We just try and live the way Father tells us. I don't know what sort of a punishment he could deliver. The death penalty was abolished centuries ago, and there are no prisons today, at least none that I know of. I think he'd... correct me."

"*Correct* you?" Alb blinked, at the same time automatically nodding for a new page on the screen. He hadn't looked away from the screen once during their entire conversation. "How?"

"Well, there are still hospitals," Cassique said. "They have drugs, lasers and the like."

"You're talking about brainwashing?" Beta D asked.

"I'm talking about lobotomy," Cassique replied. Then he felt his temples with his fingers and gulped loudly. "I think the dosser would fry me," he squeaked.

Having left the office, the three sat together on the large, soft couch in the living room, hands on their knees. Nobody had said anything for almost half an hour. Cassique was staring blankly ahead, contemplating a lobotomised future, one of scrambled brains and inane, vacant grins. Alb and Beta D took turns leaning across to check the dilation of his eyes, waiting for a sign that he might be coming out of his shock. Every so often one or the other would give him a poke or a pinch and check for a reaction.

"Maybe we should throw a bucket of cold water over him," Beta D said.

"I think a small electrical shock would be better," Alb mused aloud.

"Why not combine the two?" Beta D suggested. "Douse him with water, then zap him with a few volts?"

"The holding pens!" Cassique suddenly shouted, leaping to his feet and giving the two younger men brief heart palpitations. He began striding around the space in front of them, unaware of his surroundings. "I'm going to take you back to the holding pens. I'll freeze you and stick a note on your files saying *Do Not Disturb Until The Year 3000*, and I'll walk away and return to my life and incinerate that damn hard drive and everything will be normal again and Father will never know and I won't have my brain destroyed. Come on! On your feet! Move it! Move!" He turned on his two associates and tried rousing them, but they didn't budge.

"You'd better take it easy," Beta D said calmly, "or you'll burn up those precious brain cells of yours all on your own. Don't have a cow, man, as the old saying goes."

"Cow?" Cassique snorted. "There are no cows here. No cows, no sheep, no goats, no chickens – I saw the last one before it died – and soon, no *you*!" He began to laugh.

"He's lost it," Beta D said to Alb. "He's had a breakdown."

"I have to agree," Alb sighed. "Unfortunately, a blathering idiot hardly bodes well for the pair of us, does it?"

"Hmm. I hadn't considered that."

"If he goes," Alb noted, "we go with him."

"You're right," Beta D scowled.

"We could do with that bucket of water now," Alb said.

Water didn't run to the sink in Cassique's folly of a kitchen, but the house was fitted with an ancient, working bathtub, a relic of the former owner's, who'd been one of the few humans left who enjoyed bathing in fresh water. Most people, even the out-of-sorts Cassique, preferred a dry-clean from Father while they slept or visited the realities, but there were a few who clung to the habits of the past, so water was kept on tap in certain residences.

Beta D found a large vase in one of the side-rooms which was just right for his purposes. He filled it as quickly as he could – water flowed much slower through the faucets than it used to in his day – and brought it carefully back to the main room, taking great pains not to spill any.

"Sit him down," Alb said, taking the vase, and Beta D gently manoeuvred Cassique back onto the couch. He was still blabbering.

"I'm a good Fixer," he was saying. "One of the best. Ninety-four percent success rate. Doing my bit to keep the closure on schedule. Doing it well. Father will understand. He won't hold my transgression against me. I bet he'll be amused by it all. We'll have a good laugh together while we're putting the two of you back on ice, and he'll explain why I've been feeling so tense lately, and he'll wipe all my worries away in the blink of –"

Alb tipped the vase upside down and sent the water splashing over Cassique's head, soaking him from top to bottom.

Cassique froze. His lips moved once or twice, tasting the water, but apart from that flicker he sat solid as a statue of a Buddha. He'd dipped his legs in water once, decades ago, and had found the liquid repulsive and vile. He had no trouble drinking the stuff, but as far as immersing oneself in it... He'd shuddered at the thought many times over the years, as he watched people in the past happily splash around like clumsy seals that he'd seen once from the side of a yacht.

After a lengthy pause his head swivelled slowly, and he shot Alb a questioning look. "Why?" he asked softly.

"You needed it," Alb replied.

"I needed a wash?" Cassique frowned.

"You needed a shock."

"Couldn't you have kicked or stabbed me or pulled out some of my pubic hairs?" Cassique complained. "Did you have to be quite this brutal?"

"Frankly, yes," Alb said. "Our time here is limited. We can't afford expansive recovery programmes and gradual progression. We need you compos mentis *now*, fully functional and composed."

"I can fill the vase again, if you'd like," Beta D said.

"No!" Cassique yelled. "I'm composed! I'm composed." He shook his drenched arms in disgust and spat the foreign water out of his mouth. "And, if you can dry me out within the next ninety seconds, I might even give you a chance to explain yourselves before I ship you back to the holding pens for the next few thousand years."

It took much longer than ninety seconds to dry Cassique. There were no towels in the house and, since they provided homes for disease-carrying parasites (some microscopic organisms had survived the great cleansing) and had been outlawed for more than two centuries, no bedclothes either. Indeed, there were no beds — in the twenty-ninth century one slept naked on jets of warm, soothing air. Cassique could have asked Father to turn those on, but then he'd have had to try and explain how he'd got soaked. In the end they used his spare suit, the one he kept for special occasions.

By the time the last drops had dried he was back to his usual good self. He was even starting to see the funny side of the episode, though he wouldn't welcome a repeat in a hurry. He removed the trousers from around his head and lay them with the other wet clothes near his virtual bed. He'd sleep with them next to him that night and they'd dry over the warm air and be ready again by morning.

Alb stared at Cassique's naked body and pulled a face. "Have you people no sense of shame?" he asked.

"What?" Cassique looked down at his exposed frame and laughed. "Oh, that. I forgot you hail from a nude-free time. It's just a penis and a pair of testicles, Alb. All men have them, and a good number of our non-binary citizens too."

"Non-binary?" Alb blinked.

"Trust me, that's a conversation for another time," Beta D murmured.

"Alright," Alb said. "I know it's only anatomy, but still..."

"Still what?" Cassique asked.

"It's not proper to flaunt one's genitalia this way," Alb huffed.

Cassique laughed again and flapped his privates at the great genius of the past, who turned his head away sniffily and silently admonished the barbaric people of his future.

"If you're through playing with yourself," Beta D said drily, "we've got some serious discussions to be getting on with, remember?"

"Yes, I remember." Cassique patted his penis back into place and sat down on one of the chairs opposite the couch. After a few seconds, taking Alb's offended sensibilities into account, he crossed his legs and mostly shielded the slumbering member from the stuffy young man's sight. "Now," he said, "what are we going to do about this illegal hacking?"

"You said it wasn't illegal," Beta D objected. "In a world without clear and acknowledged laws..."

"Point taken," Cassique said, rolling his eyes, "but you know what I mean. It's not, to borrow Mr Einstein's terminology, *proper*. I'm pretty sure that Father will be furious if he finds out what you two – and, by extension, my good self – have been up to. I'm not sure what will happen to me in that instance, but it'll certainly be back to the pens with you, and this time you'll stay there indefinitely."

"So don't tell him," Alb said shortly.

"It's not that easy," Cassique groaned. "You know it's not."

"It's easy if you try," Beta D sulked, unconsciously echoing the lyrics of a long-forgotten twentieth century song. "Just keep your mouth shut, go about your business as usual, and who'll ever know?"

"Father will," Cassique said.

"How?" Beta D retorted.

"He just will!" Cassique snapped. "You've been lucky so far – OK, it hasn't just been luck, you've been very clever with your hacking – but eventually you'll trigger a response somewhere and he'll be onto you. And when he gets onto you, he'll get onto me. I'm responsible for the pair of you, so if you do anything wrong, I'll have to answer for it."

"Pretend you didn't know what we were up to," Beta D said.

"Which you didn't, until just now," Alb pointed out.

"I can't," Cassique said. "I'm no good at lying. Besides, Father would see through any lies in an instant. He's got every psychological and behavioural book ever written on file in his memory banks. He can spot a guilty tic from a million miles away, if he's looking for one."

"Hmm. He has a point there," Alb said.

"In that case join us," Beta D said. "If you're guilty by association, you might as well fully associate. Throw in your lot with us and help."

"Help you?" Cassique frowned. "How?"

"Help us search the files," Beta D said. "Help us come up to speed with what's been happening in the world. Help us understand this time travel business. Fill in the blanks."

Cassique stared from Beta D to Alb and noticed them shifting uncomfortably under his gaze. "To what end?" he asked softly. "What are you searching for? It's not just information, is it? You want more. You want… what? Tell me now, and be truthful, or I'm turning you in. I mean it."

Beta D looked at Alb and raised his eyebrows. Alb hesitated, then nodded.

"We want to stop it," Beta D said. "We want to return to our own times and put an end to this abduction business. It's wrong, Cassique. It's harmful. You and your people have no right coming back like you do, ripping our lives away from us, bringing us here for observation, or just to sit on ice for the rest of time. We're human beings, like you, and we deserve the same rights. We're going to try and put a stop to Father and time travel."

"Put a stop to Father and...?" Cassique laughed. "How?"

"We don't know yet," Alb said quietly. "That's why we need *you*."

"You don't understand." Cassique shook his head and smiled bitterly. "What you're proposing is lethal. Not just to us, but to your people as well. We don't bring you here for Historians to study. That's a bonus, our attempt to make the most of the situation, but it's not the main reason, or anywhere near it. We bring you here because history dictates that we must."

"You're right," Alb said. "We *don't* understand. How can we, when nobody tells us what's happening? Explain why you have to bring us here. Tell us more about time travel and why you believe it's necessary to alter the past the way you're doing."

"I can't," Cassique moaned. "Father –"

"Father be damned!" Beta D yelled. "I'm sick of being bossed around by that computer! You've crossed him already by letting us have our own way. You've crossed him by not turning us in the second you saw what we were up to. You've crossed him by daring to be human, by questioning the way he's running and ruining this world. There's no going back. A dictator brooks no challenge. He'll eliminate you if he discovers your treachery. Whether with lasers or a stout rope, the end result will be the same. Your only hope is to join us, help us plan an escape, ideally blow up the time portals as we go, and travel back with us and hide in the past where he can't find you. It's the only way."

Cassique sneered. "It's no way at all."

"Why?" Alb asked.

"You're living in a dream land," Cassique said.

"Why?" Alb asked again.

"It can't happen," Cassique insisted. "What you're suggesting is impossible."

"Why!" Alb jumped up and darted forward to grasp Cassique's arms. Cassique flinched at the contact and almost vomited. "Why won't it work?" Alb growled. "Why is it impossible?" He shook the older man furiously. "For heaven's sake, tell us. Let us know what we're up against. Give us a chance, man. For the love of God, give us a *chance*."

Cassique's eyes closed, and he took a deep breath. Alb released him and slowly sat down again. Beta D leaned forward eagerly.

Cassique's eyes opened, and they were steady and clear, the gaze of a man who had come to peace with his inner demons. "Very well," he said in a low, scared croak. "I'll tell."

SIX

Cassique was still sitting on the couch, but Alb and Beta D had brought through chairs from the dining room and were seated opposite him. Although it gave the conversation something of the feel of an old-style police interrogation, they all instinctively felt it would be easier this way.

"Where do you want me to start?" a weary, shaken but resigned Cassique asked. "How much do you want to know?"

"Everything," Alb said.

"I don't know *everything*," Cassique sniffed. "Even experienced Fixers like me possess limited knowledge, just enough to make sense of what we're doing, but no more than that. I can explain what time travel is, and, to an extent, how it's been achieved, but if you want a blow-by-blow account…"

"A general overview will do for a start," Alb said, offering Cassique a smile of support. "When did your people start going back in time?"

"2680," Cassique replied promptly, sure of that date at least.

"A hundred and seventy-three years ago?" Alb whistled appreciatively.

"By the Prophet's teeth," Beta D scowled. "You've been stealing people for close to two centuries?"

"I wouldn't call it stealing, exactly…" Cassique began, but Alb waved away the distinction.

"Was that why they went back?" Alb asked. "Did they do it specifically to take people out of their timelines, or were they explorers who, at first anyway, only wanted to see how people had lived in the times before theirs?"

"They were explorers," Cassique said, managing a weak smile, glad that Alb could understand at least this much about them. "It was the final great spurt of the flame of human inquisitiveness. They wanted to explore new frontiers, unlock the secrets of the universe, that sort of thing. We'd given up on space, and there was little in the world of our own time that was strange or a challenge to us, but the realities and sex spas hadn't at that point entirely claimed the minds and souls of the population. There were humans who worked in tandem with Father, geniuses bent on prying open the final panel of Pandora's Box — they wanted to conquer time. They saw an opportunity to go into the past and they took it.

"What most motivated them?" he mused aloud. "Did they wish to change the present by tinkering with the past, or did they hope to learn more about the origins of our universe? I don't know. Perhaps both of those reasons, perhaps neither of them. Why did the people of the twentieth century invent the nuclear bomb? They knew about its destructive capabilities, that they could be condemning the planet and their children to complete obliteration, but they went ahead anyway."

"Time travel is destructive?" Beta D blinked.

"They toyed with the dynamics of time," Alb said. "Of course it's destructive. How could it be anything else? I'm just surprised the destruction isn't already upon us."

"It will be," Cassique said. "Soon. If we fail."

"*Fail?* What do you..." Alb stopped and gathered himself. "We're jumping too far ahead. Backtrack a bit. Forget motives and knock-on effects. *How* did they do it? How did they open, as you put it, that final panel of Pandora's Box?"

Cassique took a few moments to compose his words. "Time," he said when he was ready, "is like the water of a deep lake. If you look at it from above, all you see is the surface. That is what we call the present, and until 2680 the surface – the present – was all we could ever see, all we could ever experience.

"Now, penetrating the surface of water is no problem for us," he went on. "We can simply stick in a limb. We can dive down through it. We can build machines to take us to the very bottom of a body of water if we so wish, yes?"

Alb and Beta B both nodded, their expressions rapt.

"But some creatures can't," Cassique said. "In your time, you had insects who lived on the water's surface. They moved across it as though it was impenetrable. As far as those insects were concerned, it was a wall, as solid as anything either of you could imagine. To those tiny creatures, the idea of burrowing beneath the surface and into the water would be absurd. How could one pass the impassable? It was a barrier, a floor, a full stop.

"Well, as those insects were to water, so were we to time. We skimmed the surface of the ages, never diving into the past times, thinking it impossible, if we thought about it at all. Writers would occasionally play with the notion, like an infant might play with a games console, enjoying the lights and noises, but never really understanding or controlling what they were playing with.

"Until the twenty-seventh century." He paused to lick his lips. "That was when we discovered a way to break through the surface of time. We blasted through. Our device was a descendant, in a way, of the nuclear missiles you helped develop." He nodded at Alb, who was surprised to find himself linked to such a weapon, but he let it pass, not wanting to distract Cassique. "What Father and his team did, as far as I've been able to discern, was somehow generate an explosion which blew a hole in the surface of time, all the way back to about the year 3000BC. In effect, they took a nuclear bomb and linked it to temporality, and with it they blew a hole through the present, into the past."

"*Blew a hole?*" Beta D echoed sceptically. "How can you blow a hole in time? It's not physical."

"In a way, it is," Cassique said. "If you look at it from the correct angle, it's physical and viscous, just like the surface of water can be."

"The power involved must have been monumental," Alb commented.

"I think it drained almost every source of electrical energy on the planet," Cassique agreed. "Father doesn't admit as much, but I get the impression he almost went down with the explosion. It took a few decades to replenish all the energy banks worldwide."

"But you've learned to control the explosions now?" Alb asked. "It's easier to blast into the past these days?"

Cassique shook his head. "There have been no further explosions."

Alb frowned. "But then how do you travel back?"

"Through the Time Hole. The hole the initial bomb created is still open."

Alb's face nearly exploded with shock. "After all this time?" he gasped.

"Yes," Cassique said.

"A bomb's effect lasting almost two centuries? Impossible!" Alb said.

"Not at all," Cassique countered. "If a normal bomb explodes on Earth and creates a hole, the space it leaves in the ground remains indefinitely. Eventually it will get filled in, as all holes do, with dust and dirt and shifting soil and pebbles, but it can last a long time, long after the final reverberation of the bomb's blast has faded. Well, the hole in time is similar. It will, in the end, if we leave it to its own devices, collapse of its own accord, but until then it remains open, a gaping wound through the fabric of time."

"Hmm. What sort of a bomb was it?" Alb asked. "And how did –"

Cassique cut him short with a curt shake of a hand. "I don't know," he said. "I don't know how they made it, or how they connected it to time, or how it worked. I repeat, I have access to very few technical details. I'm not a scientist, and even if I was, I doubt Father would reveal much more to me. While he's still assisted in his work by teams of humans, he's far more isolated at the head of the time project – of all projects, really – than he was back then. His powers have grown over the last couple of centuries, while humanity's have diminished. He tells us as much as he has to, when he has to, but no more, and doesn't invite any questions."

Alb looked disgruntled, but he was sure Cassique was telling the truth, so he didn't press any further. "Then tell me, what effect did the bomb have on the past? I assume it wasn't as harmless as its builders had imagined?"

Cassique snorted sourly. "For a time, they thought everything would be fine. They'd been afraid the present would vanish after the explosion, but it all ticked along as before. The present carried on as it always had. The blast was declared a resounding success, and they moved quickly onto stage two."

"Stage two? Now why don't I like the sound of that?" Beta D asked with a dark, cynical chuckle.

"Stage two was their experimental phase," Cassique said. "They altered things in the past. Like, introducing manned flight a century earlier than it should have happened. Preventing the start of World War II. Aggravating the Cold War, to see what would happen when a few nuclear missiles were launched in the 1980s. Stuff like that. They figured they could always return to a point where they'd intervened and change things back to the way they'd been, if any of their tests appeared to be having an adverse effect on the present."

"But they couldn't, right?" Beta D snorted, anticipating the worst.

"Actually, they could," Cassique said.

"They could?" Alb sounded surprised.

"Yes. So long as the Time Hole is open, the past is flexible. If we go back and make a change, a new timeline opens up and its future from that point can be *very* different to ours, but it won't have any impact on our timeline – Present Time – until the Hole closes. It's like… Remember the early personal computers?" he asked Beta D. "The models that were manufactured in the twentieth and twenty-first centuries, where you could open a couple of tabs at the same time if you were browsing the web?"

"I saw a few of those in museums," Beta D nodded.

"Well, time is similar. Let's say Present Time is the original tab, the one that popped up as soon as the browser of time was opened by the Big Bang. When you open a new tab by going through the Time Hole, you can mess around all you want within it, but that won't change anything in the first tab, understand?"

"I get you now," Beta B beamed, though Alb still looked confused. "So, the past, when you travel backwards and make changes, becomes another tab, one that sits alongside the tab of your own time but doesn't impact on it?"

"Exactly," Cassique said.

Beta D smiled at a deeply puzzled Alb. "Never mind," he said. "I'll explain the web and browsing to you later. It's not as complicated as it sounds, just a more basic version of what we've been doing with Father's files."

"I hope you're right," Alb replied rather tetchily.

Beta D frowned and scratched an ear. "You said you could correct changes?"

"Yes," Cassique said. "At any stage we can return to the other timeline around the point where we made a change, then negate that change. To give an example, in one of our early experiments we scuttled Christopher Columbus' ships, so that the Americas wouldn't be discovered by Europeans in 1492. We then proceeded to visit the alternate timeline at various points over the following thirteen hundred years, studying that world and noting how it differed from ours.

"When we tired of the experiment, we returned to the day when we knocked holes in the ships' hulls and repaired them. That allowed Columbus and his crew to set sail as before, meaning that timeline now aligned exactly with our own. We then went back to a different period, changed something there, studied how that altered the course of history, then went back and rectified that change. And so on."

Beta D's frown deepened. "If the changes you make in the past don't harm your Present Time, where's this problem that you've been speaking of? You said the world was facing destruction if you failed. But fail to do what?"

"I'm coming to that, if you'll give me a chance," Cassique chided him.

"Sorry," Beta D said, flashing him the peace sign. "Please, continue."

Cassique shifted about on the couch, making himself more comfortable, before picking up the thread again. "While the alternate timeline doesn't affect us as long as the Time Hole remains open, it would if the Hole ever closed before the past could be put back the way it was. We're not absolutely certain – it's not the type of experiment you can carry out in a lab – but as far as we know, if the Hole closes and the past's not the same as it originally was, the present as we know it will be wiped clean. Father reckons that the explosion will rip back to the moment of alteration, erasing every temporal period since then, and time will start anew from that point."

"Huh?" Beta D's face was blank, and this time it was Alb's turn to smile. He could see what Cassique was leading up to, and he laid out the scenario before Cassique could, in a clearer and more poetic way than Cassique would probably have managed.

"It's simple, my friend," he said. "Think of that occasion when they sabotaged Columbus' ships. If the Time Hole collapsed before they could return and repair the craft, all the events after that point would cease to be. As the hole collapsed, time itself would retract. I imagine it would be like a rain of white fire streaking backwards from here to 1492, destroying all in its path.

The fire would stop at the moment of change, leaving the past before that point intact, and present time would start all over again from there."

"So, the present – Cassique's *now* – would never have been?" Beta D asked.

"This present, your present and my present," Alb nodded. "All of the presents since Columbus' discovery of the American continent... gone. In the Columbus scenario, if the Time Hole collapsed this instant, everything would snap back to 1492, and that's where the world would start over, its people progressing towards a new future in the course of natural time."

Beta D blinked. "Then all the billions of people who've lived since then would be obliterated? They'd all be lost?"

"In a way, yes," Cassique said, taking over again. "In another way, they'd never have existed in the new timeline, so you could argue that they couldn't actually be lost. It's like our actions today — every move we make creates a future, which becomes the only real future as we move into it. When we make a choice in life, discarding one possible route for another, we close the door on dozens or hundreds or thousands of potential futures. Are we then to be held responsible for the lives which will never exist in those abandoned futures because of our choices? Of course not. This isn't so different. The people of the fifteenth century would know nothing of a changed future, or all the people who'd been *lost*. Our future is what we make it, and theirs is the same."

"But we're not talking about the future," Beta D protested. "It's the past."

"To us, yes," Cassique said, "but in this new past world, which would be the only world left, it wouldn't be. It would be the present."

"Shit, this is too confusing for me." Beta D stood. "I'm going for a piss. Maybe that'll help me think straight. It normally does."

He left the room and relieved himself. There were no toilets in the houses of the twenty-ninth century, as there was no shame attached to defecation anymore. One merely called for Father when needs required, and suction tubes appeared from pretty much any wall or floor, followed by wipes, towels and whatever else might be needed. Cassique thought nothing of passing urine and solids in front of his guests, but there were some habits Beta D and Alb could not and would not break, so they excused themselves whenever necessary and retired to see to their business discreetly.

Beta D felt better when he returned, refreshed. Ignoring his chair, he flopped onto the couch next to Cassique and sighed happily. "I knew that would do the trick. It feels like a great weight's been lifted. So, Cass, listen." He leant forward and joined his hands contemplatively. "We still haven't got to the heart of the matter, have we? If going back in time is a cinch, and changing the changes is fine and dandy... You see where I'm heading?"

"Of course," Cassique smiled. "You're asking me, again, where's the problem? And in theory there shouldn't be one. We hadn't been certain, going into the experiment, what the effects of changing the past would be. There was no way of knowing for sure. We had to mess about with the past a few times before we were sure that it couldn't harm us. When Father was through judging the dangers and pitfalls, he decided it was OK to continue to go back and make changes, so long as we put things right fairly swiftly in Present Time."

"I'm not sure I follow," Beta D said.

"We can leave the altered timeline open for hundreds, even thousands of years as the people in that other *tab* experience time," Cassique explained. "We can re-enter it at any point, any number of times, between when it opened and where it stands today. So, with that Christopher-Columbus-didn't-discover-America experiment, the team came back to our present, then returned to the other timeline a hundred years down the road from 1492 to check what was happening with the world. They popped back every hundred years or so after that, all the way up to the present day, to see how things were going and how that world differed from ours, but they did all that in a couple of days of Personal Time, as they only stayed in the other timeline for a few minutes of Present Time whenever they entered it. At the end of those two days, they went back to 1492, fixed the ships, and all was as it had been again. The altered timeline existed for more than thirteen hundred years of its own time, but only forty-eight hours in our present."

"I thought they would have wanted more time to study the consequences of their changes," Alb said. "They can't have learnt much in that short a period, spending just a few minutes in that timeline every century."

"Oh, the time travellers stayed there for months, even years, of their Personal Time," Cassique said. When he saw the pair's confusion, he swiftly elaborated. "When we enter the past, we experience time the same way that people of the period we're in experience it. If we stay there for ten years, we age ten years.

We call the time we spend in a past timeline, Personal Time. But only a fraction of that passes in what we refer to as Present Time. So if we spend a month of Personal Time on a mission in the past, only a few minutes of Present Time will have elapsed when we return."

"That's a head-scratcher," Beta D muttered, "but I think I get it. So, with the Columbus example, let's pretend for simplicity's sake that the team had limited their observations to three centuries, and visited that timeline for a month in each century to check that everything was going OK. For the people in that timeline, three hundred years would have passed. For the Fixers, three months would have passed, and that's how much they'd have aged. But here in the present, only three days would have ticked by for everybody else. Is that about the sum of it?"

"It's not that neat," Cassique smiled, "but yes, that basically sums it all up, relatively speaking." He winked at Alb, whose theories had been central to the unlocking of the portals of time, then continued with his account of time travel's early years. "Experimental trips to the past ran around the clock, one mission after another, headed by different teams. There were so many time periods that Historians wanted to tinker with. Some wanted to go back only a few decades or centuries to carry out controlled experiments, looking at what would happen if you made very minor changes in a very specific field, while others were interested in going back a few thousand years and making sweeping changes which would affect the whole of civilisation. The Historians were keen to squeeze in as many missions as possible, as fast as they could, as they knew the clock was ticking and the Time Hole would collapse at some point in the not-too-distant future."

"You're utterly sure it won't remain open indefinitely?" Alb interrupted.

"One hundred percent positive," Cassique said. "Father can hasten its closure – he plans to shut it down before it closes naturally, once we've corrected all the timelines – but he's never found a way to bolster its walls and keep it open for longer. He estimated, a few years after the explosion, that we had approximately two centuries of Present Time to play with. Somewhere around that point, as closely as he could predict, the strain on the sides of the Time Hole would force it to close."

"Strain?" Alb was focussed intently on Cassique. "Where does this *strain* come from?"

"From time," Cassique answered. "The Hole penetrates time, clean through to 3000BC, but only in one spot. It's like… You've heard the story of Moses?"

Alb blinked, thrown by the sudden change. "Of course."

"I think so," Beta D said, less certainly. "Wasn't he the guy in those twentieth century movies, with the beard and the long hair?"

"Those were actors," Cassique told him. "The real Moses – I mean the mythical one, as he didn't actually exist – was a man who led a race of people known as the Israelites out of a place called Egypt, where they were slaves."

"He was kind of like Spartacus?" Beta D asked.

"Kind of," Cassique agreed, ignoring the guffaw of disbelief from Alb. "One of the things he supposedly did, while leading his people to safety, was part a sea. Legend has it he lifted his arms or struck the sand or something, and a path opened up in the sea in front of them, and that was how they escaped."

"I remember now," Beta D said.

"Oh, you do, do you?" Alb shook his head despairingly. "If this is the face of my world's future, I'm glad you took me when you did."

"Yeah, I know it," Beta D went on, ignoring Alb's friendly jibes. "That was the one where the sea divided. There were walls of waves to either side, held back by magic, but the walls fell when the baddies followed, and they all got drowned. I saw that when I was a nipper. A great old film."

"Well, I haven't seen the movie," Cassique said, "but roughly speaking that's what the hole through time is like. It divides the temporal sea but only for a while. All the time the walls are coming under immense pressure from the *waves*. One day the walls will crumble, and the sea of time will rush back in to fill the gap, and everything will be the same as it was before. You understand?"

"Sure," Beta D said.

"Yes," Alb responded.

Cassique paused once more as he contemplated the next part of the story. "For a few decades we thought all was good. We had a hole in time which we could pass through, a couple of centuries to play around with it, and no problems so long as we crossed our i's and dotted our t's whenever we were done testing any given timeline, to ensure the changes were negated and couldn't come back to haunt us when the Time Hole shut."

"But there were complications?" Alb guessed.

"Dos, yes," Cassique groaned. He passed a hand over his eyes, shook his head grimly and pressed on. "We began to notice, as we went about our business in the past, that things were *different* in certain eras and places. History had changed. We'd go back to a certain date to experiment with an Einstein or a Beta D and find they weren't the way they should be, that Einstein hadn't come up with the theory of relativity when he should have, or Beta D had killed himself after his accident with a computer game. Stuff like that.

"The past had changed in many places and it no longer corresponded with our original history records. The more we travelled back and looked around, the more discrepancies we found, people out of synchronisation with their histories. The Egyptians hadn't built the pyramids. The Confederates won the American Civil War. The apple didn't drop on Newton, even figuratively speaking. Shakespeare got a job on a farm and never wrote any plays. James Dean survived his car crash and went on to make more than a hundred films that were so mediocre, nobody cared to watch the first few good ones that he'd starred in. And so on.

"We thought that our tinkering was to blame, that this had happened because of changes we'd made during our experiments, that we hadn't rectified them as neatly as we'd assumed. We went over and over the records of our trips to the past, looking for the slips that we must have missed, but there weren't any. We'd been as clean and efficient as we'd believed. The changes we'd made weren't the root cause of the fractured past.

"Then we thought, maybe it was a result of people from *our* future, travelling back as we were, and their messing about in the past had resulted in the… well, the mess."

"That couldn't happen," Alb said shortly. "No, impossible." He shook his head vehemently. "A time hole could only stretch back from the present in which it had been created. The future can't exist at the same time as the present. Unless *they* had come back in time, to *your* time, through one time hole, and opened another in your present..."

"No, you were right first time," Cassique said. "Our future selves had nothing to do with the scrambled past. Father could find no evidence of a time hole from the future into our present and dismissed the notion. Besides, the only being on Earth who fully understood how to create such a time hole was Father, and he'd determined never to open another one again.

"So, we studied the matter further. We went through all the options one by one, discounting alien influences, future intrusions, parallel universe theories, wrongly recorded historical accounts — we thought maybe the records that had passed down to us had been rewritten centuries before, by one oppressive regime or another. We were thorough in our search. We couldn't afford to dismiss any possibility, no matter how crazy or improbable it seemed. In the end, when we'd discounted everything else, it turned out the answer was embarrassingly simple.

"The explosion itself was the source of the disruptions." He beamed at the other two, who simply stared at him blankly. "The explosion changed history," he said, trying to make them understand. "The shock waves it created swept back through time and altered the past."

"In what way?" Alb asked.

"In hundreds of thousands of ways," Cassique answered. "It didn't change the entire past, only sections of it. You can think of it much the same as the damage inflicted on a group of people who are standing on the perimeter of an ordinary bomb blast. The blast won't kill all the bystanders, but it can damage body parts, puncture eardrums, blind eyes, rip off a limb or two here and there.

"The time explosion wreaked a similar kind of damage. The shock waves didn't destroy the past — there'd be no hope for us if they had — but they wounded it. They randomly changed certain events and people. In this new, shaken past, the Russians were first to the moon. The British fell to the Spanish Armada. Ronald Reagan won an Oscar and stayed in movies. Bill Gates didn't quit Harvard or found Microsoft. You follow?"

Beta D pulled at an earlobe, uncertainly. He shot Alb a questioning glance, but the greatest mind of its time was looking inward as it mulled the matter over.

"History has changed?" Beta D finally asked.

"Parts of it, yes," Cassique said.

"Only parts?" Beta D pushed. "Surely, if one block goes, all the others must tumble too."

"Not blocks," Cassique said. "*Tabs.*"

"Tabs, blocks, what's the…" Beta D winced. "Oh, hold on…"

"Tabs exist independently of one another," Cassique finished the thought for him. "When Father opened the Time Hole, the past experienced the aftershocks simultaneously, which basically opened up hundreds of thousands of different time tabs, and history is unfolding independently in each of those tabs, but at the same time as in every other tab, and in isolation from them.

"Let's take two different leaders in time," Cassique said, trying to make it easy for his charges. "Julius Caesar and…" He'd been about to say Donald Trump, but Alb would have no idea who that was, and the explanations would have taken too long and taxed his credulity. "Otto von Bismarck. When the Time Hole opened, one of the tweaks imposed on history was that Caesar wasn't assassinated. He heeded his wife's warning, stayed at home that day and lived another twenty years. Nearly nineteen hundred years later, a teenaged Bismarck cut his foot on a nail, it got infected, and he died.

"Both of those changes had seismic, far-reaching consequences, and changed the future of their timelines indefinitely, but from our viewpoint they happened *at the same time*. Hundreds of thousands of alternate timelines were created, which means hundreds of thousands of different histories are unfolding even now beyond the walls of our Time Hole, but their points of origin remain embedded in *our* past. Thus, if we go to the 1840s to push young Otto out of the way of the nail that was going to seal his fate, we find a world where Julius Caesar *was* killed, and where the Egyptians *did* build the pyramids, and where Montezuma *didn't* have Cortés beheaded."

"History has been punctured in hundreds of thousands of different points," Alb murmured, "but all those punctures were inflicted at the same moment, so the earlier changes have no influence on the time periods where the later changes are taking place."

"Exactly," Cassique nodded. "The changes haven't affected our present and won't until the Time Hole closes. They've had knock-on consequences, and created their own parallel versions of history, but none of those other-tab-pasts can disturb our present world so long as the Hole is open."

"Then it's possible to correct things?" Alb asked.

"Absolutely, if we can isolate all the discrepancies and fix them," Cassique said. "That's why we've been kidnapping people and engineering events to suit our own needs. It's not hard to fix any given hiccup in the past, but when you consider the parts as a whole... when you take the hundreds of thousands of blemishes into account... It's like a massive jigsaw puzzle, the biggest the world has ever seen, whose pieces are scattered across almost six thousand years.

"First you need to identify all the pieces, then you have to slot them together correctly. It's a mammoth task. We've been delicately balanced on a knife's edge for a hundred and seventy-three years now, aware that one simple mistake could destroy us all, having to rush to beat the unavoidable closure of the Time Hole. It looked for a long time like we weren't going to make it, that there were too many flaws for us to fix, but Father bred more Fixers, and we increased our work rate, and slowly, gradually, we've come out on top of the situation. It's been hard, it's been exhausting, but we've done it. Almost."

"The *flaws*," Alb said. "How do you recognise them?"

"We have complete history records," Cassique told him. "Father has access to every news report and historical record ever digitalised. He's merged them all to create a super-history which lists every moment of humanity's development and progress through the ages. It's the most accurate, all-comprehensive file of its type ever compiled. With that to guide us, we go back in time, compare what we find with what should be, and make any necessary changes."

"But the records could be wrong," Alb said. "History is often recorded from a position of bias. Generals exaggerate, conquerors rewrite the past, thieves take the credit for others' successes. How can you be sure that your record of the past is correct?"

"It doesn't have to be a hundred percent accurate," Cassique said. "So long as it generally corresponds, it'll be fine. For instance, in *your* later life you're credited with inventing the theory of relativity. As far as we know, that was all your own work, and you really were the greatest mind of your time. But you might not have been. Perhaps you swiped the idea from a penniless student, then slit his or her throat."

"I would never –" Alb started to protest loudly.

"I'm not suggesting you would," Cassique calmed him. "I'm merely using it to illustrate a point. And the point is, if you did steal it, if it wasn't your theory, so what? History has credited the breakthrough to you. Billions of people came to know your name and understand something – in most cases a very *little* something – of your theory, but how many knew *you*? How many people met you or spent time with you or knew your favourite joke or how you ate or how you treated your friends and relatives?" Cassique shrugged. "It doesn't matter. You could be a saint, a son of a bitch, or one of the masses in between. Nobody knows, nobody cares, and it doesn't make a jot of difference.

"The everyday world exists separately to that of time and history," Cassique continued. "People matter in life, of course, but history takes little notice of them. Moses didn't exist, so he didn't part a sea or bring the Commandments down the mountain, but he did in the historical records, and thousands of years on from when he allegedly lived and died, that's all that really matters, isn't it? The myth *is* the reality, as far as history is concerned.

"Maybe Mozart wasn't as brilliant a prodigy as reported, but we all know him as a boy-wonder. When people think of him, they think of the six-year-old entertaining the kings and queens of Europe. In reality, maybe he did and maybe he didn't, but historically he most definitely did, and when the Time Hole closes, that's the only truth that's going to matter. That's all we need to get right. The minutiae of life, the everyday world of eating and drinking and breathing and sleeping... irrelevant."

"You think so?" Alb asked.

"How could it be otherwise?" Cassique said. "A person's actions are lost to reality within seconds. Their words and deeds are forgotten and confused within minutes. Look at us three — if we were asked, an hour from now, to relate this conversation verbatim, how close do you think our accounts would match?"

"You have a point," Alb admitted.

"History is what the stories have made it," Cassique said bluntly. "Nero might not have fiddled while Rome burned, but so long as legend says he did, he did, and so long as we get the legends right, so long as we can fix the past to fit the style of the stories, we'll be OK when the Time Hole collapses. If we control the story of the past, and make sure it matches the story that was told before we punched a hole through time, we'll control reality. And that's not my view — it's history's."

They'd been talking for what seemed like forever. Cassique had never engaged in a conversation this long before. Communication was no longer a skill or a requisite in the twenty-ninth century. Father answered questions quickly, in the manner of all binary mechanisms, and the humans of the time weren't much different. As far as they were concerned, talk slowed action down and was to be avoided whenever possible. Cassique rubbed his hands over his unusually dry throat and ordered a honey-based drink which he sipped gingerly.

Alb and Beta D had moved their chairs over to a corner and were discussing the ramifications of time travel as it had been outlined to them. Cassique could see them drawing up a mental list of further questions and groaned quietly. The sun was down for the night and there was nothing he wanted more than to sleep, but he supposed he might as well stay up and see the talks through. He didn't want to be facing the pair and their questions first thing in the morning with a groggy head and bleary eyes.

When Beta D and Alb were ready, they drew their chairs back towards the couch, where Cassique was still sitting, and the interrogation resumed.

"We know you can go back almost six thousand years," Beta D said, "but can you nip back to yesterday or last week?"

Cassique shook his head. "The hole in time starts in 2680," he said. "That's the most recent point we can return to."

"How long do you normally spend in the past, on a mission?" Alb asked.

"It varies from assignment to assignment, but on average maybe two or three months of Personal Time," Cassique said. "Once an error has been identified, we fix it — which can be a matter of seconds or years — then usually move forward in time a number of times, to check that all is now good with the timeline."

"And you said a month of Personal Time in the past usually equates to a few minutes of Present Time here?" Alb asked.

"That's variable," Cassique said. "The further back you go, the more Present Time passes while you're absent. There are two reasons for that. First of all, time travel *takes* time — it's not an instantaneous process, and the further into the past you trek, the longer it takes to get there and back again. We're not talking epic journeys — it's a matter of seconds or minutes — but it all adds up.

"Secondly, although Personal Time is largely divorced from Present Time — as in, if a Fixer spends a month in the past, a month doesn't elapse here too — they *are* subtly connected on some temporal level which I don't really understand, so time does pass here too, albeit at a far slower level than the Personal Time a Fixer is experiencing while on a mission.

"To give a couple of very rough examples of how it differs, if you spend a week in AD 2000, the present will have moved on by two or three minutes when you return, but if you spend a week in 3000 BC, several hours will have elapsed."

"When you travel back," Alb said, "how fast do you go?"

Cassique smiled. "I knew you'd ask that — how could the father of $E=MC^2$ not be concerned about speed? Well, the answer is it doesn't really come into play. We don't actually move in space when we travel back in time, although our bodies do vanish out of the present."

"And how do you travel back?" Alb asked.

"Through the Time Hole," Cassique answered.

"I mean, how do you get through the Time Hole? Do you just step into it and disappear?"

"Oh. No, the Time Hole is all around us — because it's a rift in time, not space, it's not confined to any specific area — but access is limited. Father's built stations all around the planet for tapping in, and he controls all the missions."

"Run us through the procedure," Alb said. "You go to these stations of yours and…" He arched an inquisitive eyebrow.

"Well, first we're sent to a station in the general region of the place we're going back to," Cassique said. "Then we suit up. We're very careful when it comes to protection — we don't want to return with any of those old diseases of yours. We can be zapped back individually from the station, and often are when we're doing a quick check-up after we've made a change, but at the start of a mission we normally travel in a team, on a sky ship. Those ships are stocked with food, drink, and entertainment, enabling us to avoid as much direct contact with the natives as possible. When all members of the team are in place, we take our seats and wait for lift-off. When Father's ready, he orders the ship up into the sky and —"

"Father operates the ship?" Alb cut in.

"In the present, yes, but not when we're in the past. Father can't communicate directly with us once we've slipped through the Time Hole. He experimented with onboard mobile units, but they proved unreliable, so we handle things once the mission commences, though a lot of what the ship has to do is programmed into its system beforehand. When we're ready, the ship rises and moves to a safe position. Then Father shoots a stream of matter at us and we're off."

"Father does what now?" Beta D blinked, then looked at Alb. "Am I missing something obvious here? Do you know what he's talking about?"

"No," Alb said. "Please, Cassique, back up. What is this *stream of matter*? And how do you determine which part of the past you are *off* to?"

"Sorry, I forgot you don't know any of... Alright." Cassique took a deep breath. "If you think I've been vague so far, I've bad news for you, because things are about to get a whole lot vaguer. I have the basic gist of how it works, but not much more than that.

"You both understand about matter, right? Elements, atoms, molecules?" The other two nodded. "And since the twentieth century – this is after your time, Alb, so this may well be news to you – we've been able to date it. I don't know how, exactly – I've heard of a thing called carbon dating, so I assume that's how Father does it – but we can. And these days we can date it precisely. Father's able to take a sample of old plant or animal matter from any spot in the world and date it to almost the exact second that the plant or animal died. In the run-up to the opening of the Time Hole, and ever since, Father has had operatives collecting samples from all over the planet, collecting pieces of matter for pretty much every day back to 3000 BC.

"When Father wants to send someone from the present to the past, he dips into his collection and selects a sample of matter from a certain time — let's say 1456, when Gutenberg was meant to publish the first printed Bible. He then has to generate a tiny explosion in the hole made by the first, massive explosion. This minor blast sends a few shock waves down the tunnel to the past, waves you can catch and ride with the proper equipment. Father uses the matter in the explosion, in such a way that it acts as a focal point, an arrow into the past. It guides the waves back to the intended date – a specified day, sometimes even a specific hour or minute – and carries the ship and the Fixers along with it, or just a Fixer in their suit if you're flying solo. Once there, you set about doing as Father has directed you."

"And when you want to return?" Beta D asked.

"You press a button in your suit or on the ship," Cassique answered. "It sets off another blast, this time using matter from the present, and you start the journey back. It's the simplest mode of transport ever invented. A few seconds or minutes, depending how far back you're going, and you're anywhere in time you want to be. That same small amount of time when your job is finished, and you're back home for a romp in the sex spas. Simple, fast, effortless."

"Beats the local bus service, that's for sure," Beta D laughed.

"It sounds *too* simple," Alb mused aloud. "I think there's more to it than you understand. I'm sure one can't manipulate time that easily."

"You may be right," Cassique shrugged. "I'm just telling you what I know and can only pass on what I've been told. This is how Father explains time travel to us, so that's as much as I know about it."

Alb nodded slowly. "It's enough, I suppose," he said grudgingly. "It sets the scene if nothing else. You use matter from the past to invade the past... you isolate fractures in time, then correct them..." He frowned. "How can you be sure that the corrections will last? How do you know, by removing me from my timeline and replacing me with a... what are they called again?"

"Gemini," Beta D supplied the missing word.

"Yes, a Gemini. How do you know it will work?" Alb pressed. "How can you be sure you haven't missed a mistake? If you replace Gutenberg, maybe his Gemini will deliver the first Bible a week or even a day later than he should have. Such a tiny error wouldn't be all that noticeable, and probably wouldn't change the future vastly, but it should be enough to alter things to some meaningful extent. Can you be certain that you've *completely* repaired the broken past every time you go back to fix it?"

"Pretty much," Cassique said confidently. "We check each timeline thoroughly after a mission, making sure everything's going according to plan. If something goes wrong – if, for instance, a Gutenberg Gemini makes a mistake with the date of the first printing – it will register and we simply go back, swap out the faulty Gemini and fix it again. But it's rare that we have to do that. Our Geminis are well trained and utterly dedicated, and often spend decades getting ready for their assignments."

"But something as easy to miss as a tiny change in the printing date," Alb persisted. "Would you really pick that up?"

"Most probably," Cassique said. "Father doesn't miss much."

"But not definitely?" Alb asked softly.

"No, not definitely," Cassique admitted. "We can't be *definite* until the Time Hole caves in on itself, and we see what happens. But we're circumspect and each point of alteration is checked by at least five separate teams over the ensuing years, decades, and centuries. The chances of our missing even a mistake as minor as that are incredibly slim."

"Do the Geminis return to the future – your present – after they've registered their success?" Beta D asked.

"No," Cassique said. "It's the role of a lifetime, and they have to see out that lifetime. They mirror the Original's life as closely as they can, until the moment of that person's established death. At that point, they must die too, bringing their mission to its natural, mortal end."

"Couldn't you extract them before that point?" Beta D asked. "Replace them with a waxwork dummy or something at the very end? It seems cruel to put them through the whole death part, especially if the person they've replaced died young, say in an accident or something."

"It's safer and cleaner this way," Cassique said. "There was talk of extracting living Geminis in the early years of the programme, but it was decided to stick with doing it like this."

"That's brutal, man," Beta D whistled. "Forcing them to sacrifice their lives that way…"

"Nobody forces the Geminis to do anything," Cassique protested. "They volunteer for the missions and know what they're getting into. They spend years or decades training, learning to live as the person they'll be replacing. They get a full life when they go back — well, as full as the Original's was. Time passes for them the same as it does for us. They get to live as their favourite character, do everything he or she did, take the credit for every smart line, great conquest or thrilling love affair. Sure, they have to endure the pain too, the losses and humiliations, and in the end the death, but it's *their* choice. They're like actors in your times, only they immerse themselves in the roles to the point where they truly become the person they're portraying." He paused. "Many of your art critics would consider that the greatest achievement possible, I'm sure."

"Yeah," Beta D jeered, "the ones who don't have to immerse themselves in a role and die. Why do they do it?"

"You'd need to ask the Geminis that question," Cassique said, "but from what I gather, the Originals are their heroes. Taking the place of a Dante or Socrates or Genghis Khan… they see that as a prize beyond all others. Not to mention the fact that they're saving the world – this present version of it anyway –

for the rest of humanity."

"They shouldn't bother," Beta D growled. "Why sacrifice their lives for a shower of zombies who are going to spend all their time hooked up to machines in the sex spas and realities? I don't like this future world where nobody has real sex, where you can't even touch another person, and everyone does what that damn super-computer of theirs tells them. It stinks. It needs a kick up the ass to get it going again, and if I can engineer that kick – if the boots fit and I can lace them up and lift my feet to the right level – I'm just the man to fucking deliver it!"

He stopped and glared at the others. His face was red, his eyes wild, his hair fairly crackling with electricity. Cassique felt rather afraid of him, but Alb only looked thoughtful. After a few minutes he said, "You know, our young friend here might have a point." He nodded sombrely. "Yes, looking at it from the *human* side of things, he might have a very good point indeed." He paused and grinned wryly, then added, "A *fucking* good point!"

Beta D stared at Alb, shocked to hear him swearing. Then he began to laugh. Alb joined in and the two were soon howling wildly. After a while, without quite knowing why, Cassique started to laugh along with them. And, when they finished laughing, much, much later, they began to talk — or rather, to *conspire*.

SEVEN

Cassique wandered the face of his planet disconsolately. Alb and Beta D were back in the house, clandestinely hooked up to Father, cautiously circling in towards his most secret files. They didn't yet know what they were looking for, or how they could act, but their intention was clear — they wanted to bust Father and take back control of time, giving humanity another crack at determining its future. Neither was a natural hacker, but with their combined intelligence and cunning, they were proving a remarkably competent team.

Cassique wasn't sure whether to help them or turn them in. It had been easy agreeing with them the other night, when he was tired from all the talking and they made him feel part of a close-knit unit of friends. But almost a week on, he was having serious doubts. What they were proposing was the destruction of his people, his past, much of his entire timeline. And for what? Some other, alternate, unknowable world which may prove to be just as inhuman and cold as this one?

He shook his head and stared down into the waters of what had once been known as the River Shannon, on a tiny island which had been called Ireland. Most of the rivers of the world were covered over these days. The Shannon was one of the few water snakes visible from above ground, though it was uncovered only in remote, isolated stretches.

What was so bad about his time anyway? No wars, no hatred, no racism, no ugly people, no starvation, no crime, no pollution.

On the flip side...

No freedom, no free thought, no imagination, no creativity,

no say in their own affairs, no love, no warmth, no friendship, no family.

It was a case of logic versus emotion. Logically, it was easy to argue that this was the best of all times to be alive, the safest, the cleanest. People lived longer – the average life expectancy was a hundred and forty – and they no longer had to fear rape, muggings, theft, cancer, Alzheimer's, RUSH. Logically, this seemed to be an ideal world, where supply always exceeded demand, where nobody felt out of place or useless or alone, where everyone could enjoy the fruits of the planet's labour, where nobody was divided by religion, class, status, sex or race.

Emotionally, you could claim it was a dead, lost planet. What were they living for? All they ever did was play in the realities, let Father tickle their sexual fancy in the sex spas, and watch the machines do the vast majority of the work. There were no highs or lows in this world. Nothing meant anything anymore. There was almost no room for personal success or individual flair. Apart from the great drive to fix the timeline – which was purely so that the status quo could be maintained from that point onwards – there were no real challenges to be met, no enemies to be defeated, no hearts to be won or homes to be built. They existed in a sterile environment, protected against the harsh winds and savage waves which had whipped through the past, but also shielded against the warm suns and calm tides which had often warmed their ancestors and given their lives so much meaning and joy.

That was maybe the worst aspect, emotionally speaking — they could no longer look forward to change. All through history, humanity had changed and evolved. Fashions, languages (he still winced at his naïve assumption that people of different countries had spoken a single language), beliefs, and people themselves came and went, prospered and died, and the planet moved on. There was no change anymore, and no sign that there ever would be again. All they had to look forward to forever was Father, the realities, and the sex spas.

He looked for a pebble to skim across the smooth river water, but the area around the banks had been paved over centuries before. For one absurd moment he considered ripping off his clothes, diving in and swimming across to the other side. Then he decided against it. Father would clock his actions if he did – there were security cameras erected at regular intervals, to alert Father if anyone ever fell into the open stretch of the river – and questions would be asked. Besides, the water would be cold and, even more to the point, he couldn't swim.

Moving on from the river, he took a ride on one of the aeronautical supply ships and gazed down on his world from the skies. He had done this often in the past, on the time-travelling sky ships, but had never paid much attention to the planet of the present when he was in the middle of a mission to the past. His world looked clinical, grey and boring from this high up. The colours and nuances of the past civilisations were no more. The mixture of styles had been replaced with uniform structures, all designed to be functional rather than fanciful. OK, some of the buildings changed shape and colour now, which had made his visitors from the past coo, but they changed in exactly the same way in every city you visited, and any one of those cities could be swapped out with any of the others — they were pretty much identical. No matter where you went, from the banks of the

Shannon to the island once known as Japan, China to Africa, the middle of the Americas to the North or South Pole... The buildings, vehicles, and people were all the same, all part of the global unity, all one with Father's great vision.

But was that excuse enough to destroy them? Cassique pondered. Did anyone have the right to tear a world apart, just because in their view its architecture and culture had been degraded? What right had he, a mere Fixer, to say how the world should be? What right had any human?

What right has Father? a small part of him asked.

As the airship curved round into sight of the sun, he found himself dwelling on that question. What right *did* Father have? There had been objections, centuries ago, to the ever more influential role he played in the functioning of their society. People had feared this new, all-powerful computer, and had been loath to lay their lives in its invisible hands. But slowly, surely, all had come round to Father's way of thinking. Why? How? The records said they'd simply seen common sense, that the people of the planet had embraced the new way forward because it improved their lives so dramatically. Cassique had never doubted that assumption before, but now that he gave it more thought...

How much power had been handed over to Father, and how much had he usurped? His makers, programmers, and backers had been incredibly clever, some of the smartest people of their time, and they'd wielded a lot of power, but while they'd owned many politicians and civil servants, scores of soldiers and police officers, they hadn't *completely* controlled the world, its financial systems, its food supplies. Yet, in time, the computer they'd perfected did.

How?

Cassique found himself thinking about all the records Father was able to control and manipulate, and he recalled Alb saying that records could be manipulated by those with the power to rewrite them. Father had more power than any human – or group of humans – in history, and had been in power for a long time now. How easy it would have been for him, when he was only coming into that power, to change facts and figures, alter the results of votes in general elections, juggle bank accounts so that his supporters had more and his critics less.

Cassique thought about all the medicines and chemicals Father had access to. He'd taken control of the medical and pharmaceutical systems early in his reign, and all the doctors and chemists of the world had soon been taking direction from him. Physicians would use Father's incredible machines to diagnose a patient's illness, and he'd see to the quick delivery of corrective medicine or recommend surgical treatment, most of which was now carried out by his robots, whose actions he of course commanded.

Surely it would have been easy for him to misdirect some of those drugs. It would have been simple for him, for example, to poison reservoirs in countries where people were reluctant to cede power to him, or pump gas into the air at public rallies where crowds railed against his spreading influence. It would have been a relative cinch for him to kill off the bulk of his enemies with a designed disease such as, say, RUSH. To the best of Cassique's knowledge, nobody had ever suggested that RUSH might have been deliberately manufactured and released. Maybe that was because, by the time Father *helped* humanity get to grips with it, nobody of a critical nature was left to make any accusations.

Cassique had never thought like this before. He didn't know anybody in the present who had. Maybe that was part of the problem — nobody questioned any more, nobody debated or attacked or flew in the face of popular opinion. Nobody took a personal moral stand against the masses or Father. They didn't face into the wind or listen to their hearts. At least not openly. But there were those allegedly missing Fixers to account for. Had some of those challenged Father, as Cassique was thinking of doing, and was that the reason they could no longer be found?

Even if Father was guilty of the worst transgressions that Cassique could imagine, was that basis enough to shatter the timeline? If Alb and Beta D succeeded in tearing down the (arguably) tyrannical Father, they would condemn all of this present time's people to oblivion too…

Cassique thought of Nijin and Zune and how they'd rejected any of his attempts to build a true familial bond. He thought of all the people he knew in the present, all somewhat stiff, introverted, and dull, more than content to exist in their own little sealed worlds. He thought of Alb and Beta D, their eyes lighting up as their brains ignited, their indignation and fury if they disagreed with something, their love for the supposedly simpler ways of life, for intellectual pursuit, for living in harmony with the physical world.

He listened to the world now, from his vantage point in the sky, and knew that even if he had the hearing of the ancient gods, he would hear no natural laughter, no sounds of love-making, no fights which would end in tears or loving embraces. No songs to capture the imagination and move the soul. No actors (bar the Geminis) treading the boards and thrilling the crowds. No fingers clicking on keyboards or dragging pens across paper in an attempt to echo or better the great writers of the past. No painters using brushes to layer paint onto canvas and reshape the world through the lenses of their own unique viewpoints.

All he could hear, in his mind's ear, was the whirring of all the computers and machines in the realities and sex spas, the pumps bringing people to orgasm, the weak sounds of bodies shifting in large, bare rooms as their numbed minds roamed the intricate worlds of the virtual realities.

Was one really better than the other? Were the worlds of Alb and Beta D truly superior to his? Did it matter what they'd lost when they'd gained so much?

His head told him no.

His heart disagreed.

And Cassique was caught miserably between.

The airship returned to Earth and, having nowhere else to go, he returned home.

He entered the house silently and stood in the doorway of his office for a long time, watching the two young men, stolen from their timelines and bereft of their natural futures, but still hopeful, buzzing with the vitality of life, tapping buttons, scrolling down screens of numbers and figures which were an utter mystery to Cassique. They didn't speak very often, only when one wanted clarification or a second opinion.

They were compiling notes as they went, sheet after sheet of paper which they compared at the end of each day. Cassique was having a hard time keeping them supplied. Paper was rare in the present, kept in supply only for a small number of Historians who liked to use it when writing up the results of their studies. Father hadn't hesitated when Cassique asked for a few reams but had expressed surprise. Cassique told him that Alb and Beta D were bouncing various ideas off each other and promised to keep all documents for Father's later perusal, in case there was anything in them that might prove of interest to him.

Such fierce concentration was alien to the twenty-ninth century. Attention spans were shorter these days, conditioned by generations of sated instancy. Nobody had to think too much anymore or bend their brains around problems and theories. Father did all that for them. Cassique had never seen such a display of focused dedication.

Eventually he stepped fully into the room and greeted his guests. They grunted in response, noting his presence but not letting themselves be distracted by it. He sat just behind them and watched the screen flicker for a time. They were getting deeper and deeper into Father's circuits every day, uncovering details about time travel, the nurseries, the monorail routes, and Father's defence systems. They still hadn't formulated a working plan of action but felt confident that one would reveal itself soon.

"Anything new?" Cassique asked.

Alb shook his head and went on with his work. Beta D rubbed his eyes and took a break. "Nothing," he told Cassique. "Nothing that's of any use to us, anyway. We've learned lots about the food supply, how the realities work, and how he controls the sex spas, but there's nothing we can use to attack him, no way we can find of prematurely collapsing the Time Hole or blowing up the stations. There's so much in here, and it's so hard getting to the relevant information..." He shook his head in disgust. "To be honest, there's *too* much. It's crazy having it all in one place like this. If there were centres, departments, isolated memory banks... But it's all lumped together, meaning if you can pierce Father's general defences, you have access to *everything*."

"It's meant to be like a brain," Cassique said. "Father's original designers wanted their computer to mimic the human mind, in order for it to be able to think like a human."

"They did a good fucking job," Beta D spat. "Too good. I'd like to get my hands on those bastards and slap some sense into them."

"I could get one out of storage for you," Cassique suggested.

Beta D laughed. "Nah, that's OK." He paused as a thought struck him. "But I'll tell you who you *could* get."

"Who?" Cassique asked.

"*Us.*" He smiled as the thought turned. "Later versions of us exist, don't they? Me when I'm twenty-five, thirty, and so on? And Alb the same? We're not limited editions. You're able to take different versions of us from different times, right?"

Cassique nodded.

"Well, why not get older versions to help us figure out this mess? I'm sure a thirty-year-old Beta D and a fifty-year-old Albert Einstein could have Father on his knees in a matter of hours, begging for mercy."

"Maybe they could," Cassique said, "but Father doesn't allow Historians to take out more than one version of an Original at a time. Besides, your older selves are hugely popular, and I'd have to wait months, maybe years before I could get hold of one."

"Months and years which we don't have." Beta D sighed and turned back to the computer screen. "Guess I'd better just get on with it then. Could you get me something to drink, please?"

"I've decided to go through with it," Cassique said. He spoke quickly, spitting the words out before he could change his mind, making his decision in the heat of the moment, promising himself he'd stick by it, no matter what.

Beta D stared at him. "Go through with what?" he asked.

"Whatever you come up with," Cassique said. His stomach was knotted, and he found himself sweating. "If you can find a way to bring Father down, if you can change this world and set it on course for a different, hopefully more human present, I'll help you. I'll go along with you and Alb, whatever it means, however much it hurts, because I think you're right. We *do* need a kick up the arse. This world *has* gone wrong, and I want to help you change it, in the hope that we can replace it with a world where people are able to take control of their lives again."

Beta D grinned at him, then looked across at Alb, who had torn his gaze away from the screen just long enough to nod his approval and clap Cassique on the back. "And then there were three," Beta D smirked. He turned back to his work, paused, and edged over. "Here," he said, gesturing for Cassique to move forward and slot in between them. "Come closer and lend us a hand. You might as well help us now that you're with us."

"But I don't know what to do," Cassique protested.

"You'll learn," Beta D assured him. "Every human can, once they set their mind to it. Come on, I'll show you, it's easy once you get into the swing of things."

And so, trembling, hesitant at first, Cassique fully joined the plot and put his hands and mind to work against Father.

EIGHT

Cassique could feel time crumbling beneath his fingers. Each of the three men knew how close they were to their deadline. Another six days and the holiday would be over, Cassique would have to return to duty, and the Originals would be put back on ice. They still hadn't found anything to attack Father with, and while none of them had mentioned the ticking clock or the apparent futility of their search, the frustration and fear were tangible qualities clogging the air around them.

Cassique had learned fast. He was able to scroll through the data as swiftly as the other two now, although he wasn't as quick at digesting it and often had to call on them for help. He felt whole, sitting there in front of the screen, doing something meaningful with his life, following a path of his own choosing. For the first time ever, he felt truly human.

"We're getting nowhere," Beta D groaned. "This is a waste of time. I think we should reassess our goals."

"What do you suggest?" Alb asked. They were used to Beta D's pessimistic outbursts by now and knew that it was just his way of letting off steam. He was very similar to Chert in that respect.

"We're aiming too high," he said. "Look at us — a teenager, a guy in his early twenties, and a goon who only knows how to kidnap people. The three of us really believe we're sharp enough to topple history's most powerful dictator? It's a joke, man. We're kidding ourselves."

"You're suggesting we give up?" Alb murmured.

"No, not exactly," Beta D scowled. "I mean, we've got to try *something*, I get that, but maybe we should switch course. Screw

Father and this civilisation of obedient zombies. Let's look out for our own necks, junk this idea of blowing up the computer or changing time or whatever, and focus on hiding and living out the rest of our lives instead."

"Hiding," Alb repeated.

"Sure," Beta D said. "Let's work out a way to hide. I'm sure, if we work on it, we can fix things so that Father can't track us. We'll feed him misinformation, make him think we've returned to our holding pens, and hit off on the sly for some remote corner of the globe where we'll never be found."

"There are no remote corners anymore," Cassique informed him.

"Then let's fucking make some," Beta D growled.

"It couldn't work," Alb said. "I've considered it already. The holding pens are checked frequently, to ensure the Originals are in good condition. They'd find us missing within a matter of weeks, and Cassique is right, there's nowhere to go. As near as I can compute, Father would find us within two minutes, thirty-six seconds once he started looking, no matter where we holed up."

"Hiding can't be any fucking harder than short-circuiting Father or changing the past," Beta D protested.

"But it is," Alb said calmly. "Snapping a twig is a simple matter and can often be accomplished in a few seconds, but growing a tree is much harder and takes decades. Father is too sophisticated to be hoodwinked if he realises we're trying to attack or evade him. Our only hope lies in isolating a weak link and exploiting it, quickly, definitively. We can't beat him at chess, but we might be able to knock the board over and win by default."

"I hate it when you talk that way," Beta D grumbled.

Alb smiled. "Come," he said, "let's quit this yapping and get on with business, yes?" He looked over at Beta D when there was no reply. "*Yes?*" he repeated.

Beta D jerked his head sideways and grimaced. "Oh, what the fuck. Yes!"

And the simmering of their longed-for rebellion continued.

"Hmm. This is interesting." Cassique looked up when Alb spoke. "You see where I am?" he asked the others. They peered uncertainly at the screen, then he hit a button and zoomed in on the information. Cassique found himself looking at an outline of the current legal system and procedures.

"So they've got laws here after all," Beta D shrugged. "So what?"

"You see how they judge?" Alb asked.

Beta D scanned the lines of text. "Yeah. So?"

"And how they punish?" Alb pressed.

"I don't believe it!" Cassique gasped, the colour draining from his face as he made the leap ahead of Beta D. "I'd heard rumours that some Fixers had gone missing, but I'd never have connected them to anything like *this*."

"You'd heard rumours of missing Fixers?" Alb frowned. When Cassique nodded guiltily, he said quietly, "It might have been helpful if you'd informed of us this earlier."

"I had no reason to think those rumours could have tied in with what we're doing, or in such a monstrous way," Cassique croaked, starting to cry. "They were only stories that a few concerned Fixers were cautiously circulating. I didn't know any of the allegedly missing Fixers personally, so I wasn't sure whether or not I should give credence to the rumours. Even when I ran with the wild tales, as I did from time to time when I was thinking about them, I assumed that Father had merely retired the Fixers for whatever reason, set them up somewhere out of the way. In the worst-case scenario that I could imagine, he lobotomised them, as I feared he'd do to me if he found out that I was conspiring with the pair of you. I could never have guessed that he'd do such a despicable thing as this to his children. It's horrific. Those poor Fixers. To turn them into Geminis against their will... What sort of a Father... even a computerised one..."

Beta D caught up while a distraught Cassique was wiping his tears away. "Well, that's disgustingly inventive and draconically drastic," he grunted, "but I don't see what relevance it has for us. To be honest, the last thing I want to think about is what happens to us if we're caught."

"You need to read on further," Alb said, scrolling down. "You see how they decide who the conscripted Geminis replace?"

He squinted and moved in closer to the figures. "Oh, I see. Randomly generated from a core list of... We could work around that, couldn't we, and secretly arrange the selection so that we knew which one..." His eyes began to widen. "And if this is right, Father doesn't check closely afterwards. He sends a Fixer on a couple of brisk visits to the near future, to make sure all seems well, but he doesn't monitor the situation closely, as he does with timelines featuring the placement of regular Geminis."

"Why should he?" Alb asked with growing excitement. "The subjects are brainwashed and are never alive for very long. As far as Father is concerned, there's nothing they can do to adversely affect the intended unrolling of the timeline."

"Still, he'd notice if we made a big change," Beta D said, with markedly less enthusiasm.

"Yes," Alb said, "but what if we made a small one? For instance, if we managed to change Marx's *Workers of the world unite* speech a little, that might tip the scales in our favour."

"Maybe," Beta D conceded, "but we won't be able to get at Marx, will we? He's not a suitable Original for this kind of replacement."

"No, but..." Alb opened a new tab and typed in code to bring up a list of names. "If we could get to one of *these*..."

Beta D rocked gently from side to side as he considered the matter. "OK," he said, "I can see what you're suggesting, but can we exploit it? Like you noted, they're brainwashed before they're sent back. Even if we could manoeuvre one of us into such a position, what good could he do there?"

"Well," Alb said, "if we could ensure where the replacement was going – and, with your technical knowhow, I think we can probably swing that – what's to stop us from indulging in a spot of our own brain tampering, to beat Father at his own game?"

"You think we could?" Beta D sounded dubious.

Alb opened another tab and clicked a few more buttons. The article he pulled up explained how Father altered the minds and words of the punished offenders before carrying out the sentence. "I found this a week ago and kept it in mind, in case a situation arose in which it might come in useful."

Beta D began to smile.

"It would have to be me," Cassique said, once he'd read it too. He'd stopped crying and his features had hardened. Any last doubts he'd had about the direction of their mission had been wiped away by what he'd read a few minutes ago. He was all in. Father *had* to be toppled. Other Fixers had seen the same problems in the modern world as he had – he wasn't alone! – but instead of engaging with them in open discussion, Father had treated them like vermin and wiped them out. It was clear he had no regard for humanity, except in as much as humans were useful to him when they did what they were told. This was the final proof he'd needed to confirm to himself that he and his conspirators weren't overreaching, that their revolt was not only justified but essential.

Alb and Beta B looked at him soberly. "Cassique…" Alb whispered.

"He wouldn't inflict this punishment on either of you," Cassique said firmly. "He'd just stuff you back into the holding pens, ensure you're never loaned out again, and leave you there until you rot naturally a few thousand years down the line. If we go ahead with it, it'll *have to* be me."

Alb nodded slowly and switched back to the list of names again. "You know what this means?" he asked soberly.

Cassique's troubled, conflicted expression let them know that he knew exactly what he would be letting himself in for.

"Do you still think it's worth it?" Beta D asked softly. "Do you still want to help?"

Cassique looked at the names and thought about the suffering, the pain, the end. He gulped loudly, then nodded fearfully but with determination. "If you can figure out the angles," he said, voice shaking as he spoke, "I'll be your stooge. We can't let him go on doing this to people. And even though it will stop when the Time Hole closes, we can't let him get away with having done it to so many already. If we can be sure... as long as it's not in vain... I'm prepared to make that kind of sacrifice."

"Damn, you've more guts than I'd have in your place," Beta D said. "Whichever one of the Originals we pick, however we work it... It'll be nasty, man."

"I know," Cassique said hollowly.

"You're absolutely certain?" Alb asked.

He steeled himself and puffed out a weak but honest, "Yes."

"You don't want a bit more time to think about it?" Beta D asked.

"We don't have any time," Cassique sighed.

"Very well." Alb cracked his fingers and zoomed in on the list of names, so that they filled the screen. "Then let's whittle this bunch down and see what we're left with. Concentrate, gentlemen. The fate of the world's past, present, and future depends on us making the right choice today."

Beta D snorted. "I pity the poor world, then."

All three of them laughed, then put the levity to one side and seriously began considering the options at hand.

Though time was against them, they didn't rush their choice. They had to be smart, and they had to be subtle. If this was to work, they had to be surgically precise. The change they introduced had to be far-reaching and all-altering, but virtually invisible in its own self-contained moment. It was a tall order.

Finally, they found an Original they believed they could subvert. A famous man whose words had touched people in virtually every corner of the world over many centuries. He was a largely forgotten figure these days, as almost all of his ilk were in this era when the search for spiritual meaning was all but defunct, but for much of the past he'd been a global giant.

His final attributed speech, although it was written decades after his death, had been one of history's finest. Alb felt it was a shame to change it, but agreed this was their best stab at besting Father.

"As long as we keep the general meaning," he said. "We can juggle the words all we want, but we must keep the sentiment. Father's operatives will surely notice if we don't."

It was a long speech, so they set out to condense it. They didn't want to lumber Cassique with too much heavy mental baggage. It was going to be tough enough for him, struggling with the two sets of conflicting orders which the dual brainwashings would involve. The last thing he needed was a three-page script to memorise. In the end they came up with a satisfying couple of hundred words which covered most of the main ground.

The brainwashing was relatively straightforward. Father's method, perfected over the course of the centuries, involved carefully selected drugs, a stroboscope, electrical impulses, and repeated sly whispers in the subject's ear. Beta D could easily set up the lights and electricity. The only real sticking point was the drugs. They had to come up with a suitable excuse to convince Father to turn over the necessary narcotics to them without arousing his suspicions. Beta D had tried ordering them using the computer, but stopped short before executing the order when he got the sense that it would set alarm bells ringing.

Eventually, rejecting a few of the more complicated proposals, Cassique simply asked for the drugs. He told Father he wanted to experiment with his Originals. "I feel they're holding back," he said, "so I'd like to pump some truth serum into them and see what I come up with."

"That's very ambitious," Father responded. "Are you sure you want to do this by yourself? I can assign you a few experienced technicians or render assistance directly."

"I'd like to do it by myself, Father," Cassique told him. "I've come this far on my own, so I'd feel like I'd failed somehow if anyone else stepped in now. If you give me the drugs and the instructions, I'm sure I can manage."

"Very well." A few seconds later, a delivery hatch in Cassique's living room hummed and lit up. "You will take care though, won't you? These are dangerous substances."

"I'll call you the instant I run into any trouble whatsoever," Cassique vowed.

The conspirators examined the cache swiftly once Father had withdrawn. "Is everything there that we need?" Cassique asked.

"Just about," Alb said. "We don't have every last item on the list, but the base compounds are the same for both procedures, so we can mix our own solutions."

"I can't believe it was so easy," Beta D remarked, shaking his head.

"Why shouldn't it be?" Cassique replied. "I'm a responsible adult. Father trusts me."

"But simply dispensing mind-altering drugs like that..."

"The public has a right to all such substances in our time," Cassique said. "As long as you're not causing damage to anyone else, you can experiment with whatever drugs you like."

"But damage might be done to *us*, if your request was genuine," Beta D noted.

Cassique shrugged. "Originals don't count."

Beta D shuddered and began unpacking the drugs. "Come on," he said. "The sooner we blow this hellhole to smithereens, the better."

When the chemical properties were prepared and they'd treble-checked the guide, making their own sly adjustments in order to allow for the second brainwashing to come when Cassique fell into Father's clutches, they hooked Cassique up to the lights and electricity.

"Comfortable?" Beta D asked, and Cassique nodded fearfully. "Well, you won't be for long," the teenager chuckled darkly, and threw a switch.

They spent almost all the time they had left on the process. They went slowly, carefully, feeding Cassique the relevant words one by one, constructing blocks and false passages to divert Father's own programme when the time came.

"You know, we should go back and become brain surgeons," Beta D said to Alb at one point. "We'd make a fortune."

"Hush," Alb replied. "This is a delicate matter. One slip here and we'll have a human vegetable on our hands."

Cassique stared hard at the floor and tried not to tremble.

They finished with two days to spare. Alb and Beta D sat back, exhausted, satisfied they'd done all that they could. He'd sailed through three simulated tests and, while they couldn't be sure he'd pass the real one under the piercing gaze of Father, they were quietly confident.

"How do you feel?" Alb asked.

"Sore," Cassique whimpered. "My head's buzzing. It's like

it's full of bees in there."

"That should pass soon," Alb said. "It will start again when Father gets his claws into your mind, and will continue when you…" He coughed discreetly. They tried to avoid *that* subject as much as possible. "Don't worry about it. Let your thoughts wander as they will. When you get back there, it will work, or it will not. We can do no more. Go with… how do you say it, Beta?"

"Go with the flow, man," Beta D grinned.

"You're sure you'll be able to initiate the first step?" Alb asked.

"Yes," Cassique said. "That shouldn't be a problem. The opportunities in the past are endless. I'll easily find one which is believable."

"Good. And remember, it's essential you act ignorant when they bring you to trial. They must not be aware of your knowledge. Play dumb and react with shock when they sentence you. If Father suspects anything more than blind anarchy, he might dig a little deeper into your brain and that would be that."

"I'll take care," Cassique said solemnly.

"Well, that's about it then." Alb stood and sighed. He gazed around the room with more fondness than he'd anticipated. "I'm glad I got to experience this future world, regardless of the grim circumstances and no matter what comes next."

"Yeah, me too," Beta D agreed. "It's been some trip."

"It's not over yet, is it?" Cassique asked. "We've two days still to kill."

Alb shook his head sadly. "We'll return to the holding pens today."

"What?" Cassique gasped.

"We discussed it, and…" Alb hesitated.

"It's the wisest course," Beta D said softly. "We go back on ice, and you spend the next two days in the sex spas. It'll look more natural than us sticking around until the very last moment."

"But –" Cassique began.

"No buts," Alb stopped him. "It's the sensible move. Not the nicest for Beta D and me – the thought of returning to that induced sleep fills my stomach with icy dread – but I think, given the extent of the sacrifice you're about to make, it would be churlish of us to baulk at our own small discomfort."

Cassique looked from one to the other helplessly. He knew it made sense, and he knew he had to agree with their decision, but he'd miss them. They were the only true friends he'd ever known. Also, he was afraid his courage might fail him once left on his own.

He drew a deep breath. "I'll try not to let you down," he promised.

"We know you won't," Alb said.

"No freaking way, man," Beta D smiled.

Cassique paused. "If I succeed," he said, "and it goes according to plan, you two might never exist. There's no telling how the timeline will evolve, and who will or won't make the cut when it comes to the rolling out of history. Albert Einstein and Beta D could become forgotten names. Worse — they could become *never were* names."

Beta D and Alb shared a rueful look.

"We know," Beta D sighed. "The new future could go in any of a countless number of directions. We think it will follow the course of the old one up to a point, and we believe that point will lie somewhere beyond our own lifetimes. We might exist and live exactly as we did before. But we can't be certain."

"Where do you think the new future will branch from the old one?" Cassique asked, intrigued.

"When they come to time travel," Alb replied. "Everything might go the same way until then, but the collapse of the Time Hole, and the subsequent explosion we'll create if you're successful, will change the dimensions of time itself. They almost certainly won't be able to blast through the walls of time as they did in your original timeline. They may find a way to pierce the construct one day, but it won't be the same day as before."

"Then everything will be the same until 2680?" Cassique asked.

"If we're correct, the change will probably happen a lot sooner than that," Alb said. "The theoretical breakthrough came three centuries earlier, in 2391. My guess is that's the point where the paths will split definitively."

Cassique blinked, trying to remember how the world had been at that time. "In that case, Father, the sex spas, the realities... Will they all evolve the same way?" he asked.

Alb shrugged. "We don't know. Perhaps."

"Then the world could end up being just as sterile and inhuman as it is now?" Cassique cried.

Beta D snorted. "Hell, it could be even worse than before."

"But then, why are we —" Cassique started to shout.

"— bothering to try?" Beta D chuckled. "Because this way there's *hope*. We're not gods, man, we can't build an ideal society, but we can offer hope. In this new world, this new future, humans will have a second chance. Maybe this time our people will keep a closer eye on Father's development. Maybe they'll work harder to maintain control over their own lives. Maybe they'll refuse to let him become a supporting crutch and instead continue to learn and evolve and grow. Maybe this facsimile of a human world will never come to pass, and a better one, a more human one, will take its place."

"That's a lot of maybes," Cassique noted pessimistically.

"*Maybe* is all we have," Alb told him. "Father can offer certainties. We cannot. No more than our forebears could, or theirs before them, stretching all the way back to our very origins on the plains of Africa. Where humanity is concerned, life has always been a chaotic whirlpool of uncertainty."

"There *is* one other hope," Beta D said. "Space travel. That was dumped when time travel became a feasible option. Maybe now, in the new future, people will spend more time looking to the stars. That's where the real hope lies, up there." He pointed at the ceiling. "Even if Father comes to rule the planet again, he can't control space, no matter how powerful he is. If we can get up there, and find a way to soar across our solar system, and perhaps even to galaxies beyond..."

Cassique nodded. "But we three will never know, will we?"

"No one ever knows what the future holds," Alb said. Then, after a little more thought, he added quietly, "No one ever should."

He returned with them to the holding pens, dropping Alb off first, then Beta D. They maintained a formal air outside the safety of the house, saying little, giving nothing away. Cassique left them with short farewells, to which they responded likewise.

When he was back in his apartment he gave Father the details of their time together, a censored version they'd worked up for appearance's sake. He'd fed the rest – the bulk of their notes and written plans – to the incinerators. The keyboard had been unhooked and the PC screen was a useless ornament once again. And he'd returned the drugs they hadn't needed to Father.

After that he sank back on his couch, lowered his head and didn't move for five whole hours. He thought, during this spell, of Alb and Beta D, of Nijin and Zune, of Chert and Father, and all the people he'd ever known, all those he'd met with or observed in all the past times he'd ever visited. He pictured all of them wiped away, all those lives erased in an instant. He imagined himself at the centre of the temporal storm, suffering as none of the others would, as none of them ever could if they ended up not having even existed in the first place. He pictured the world starting over from the distant point he would be taking it back to if his plan succeeded, beginning again with its wars and deaths, pains and loves, losses and victories, hopes and despairs. All because of him. Billions of lives lost or lived afresh, all because of him.

His head finally lifted, and as it came up, his mouth was firmly set. "So be it," he said out loud. Then he stood and left for the sex spas. He had some living to do before he went back into the past to die.

NINE

Chert returned from the sky ship's holding pens – simpler versions of those where Alb and Beta D were stored, designed to temporarily house Originals they picked up during their missions – and rubbed hir eyes. "Father, I'm tired," ze yawned. "I feel like I'm about to catch RUSH and synapse. These treble shifts are a dossing virus."

"You can sneak a break if you like," Cassique said. "I'm still pretty fresh after my holiday, so I don't mind covering a few of your shifts for you."

"You mean it?" Chert's face lit up with gratitude. "That'd be operative! That pirate Father and his oily haste. We've loads of time left before the Hole closes. He just wants to see us scuttle for the fun of it." Chert flopped into a hammock – preferred by most Fixers to beds in the sky ships – and shut hir eyes. "I feel like I could fall asleep even without the pills," ze murmured.

"Chert," Cassique said.

"Yeah?"

"Did you ever think… Have you ever felt bad about anything you've done in the past?" Cassique spoke hesitantly.

"You mean the mistakes I've made? No. We all slot up some time. Just the way of the world."

"No," Cassique said. "I mean, have you ever felt sorry for altering the past? For letting a murderer go about their business, for putting a good man or woman down. Did you ever want to simply leave a timeline as it was?"

"Well, there *is* one thing I regret." Chert's eyes opened and ze looked worried.

"Really?" Cassique sat forward eagerly. "What?"

"Well..." Chert glanced around uneasily. "You know the *Twilight* films? Those awful vampire flicks from the early twenty-first century?"

Cassique nodded, having some vague recollection of their existence.

"Well, I was one of the Fixers responsible for making them. The Originals, in a broken timeline, decided to stop after the second film, so we had to oversee the rest of the sequels ourselves." Ze shuddered at the memory. "It still gives me nightmares. Nobody should have had to suffer those unFatherly monstrosities. Dark days, dark deeds. Still, all for the common good, right?"

"Yeah, right," Cassique answered flatly, and said no more on the subject. He should have known Chert was incapable of a serious discussion. Anyway, he'd got what he was truly after — Chert's shift. He could work alone now, for a time, and choose his moment without any hindrances.

The awkward young man seated before him was nervous and kept wringing his hands together beneath the desk. Cassique gazed once more at the sheets of paper in his lap and considered his next move.

This was the one, alright, the chance to be seized. No doubt about it. Father would come down on him like a ton of excrement for this. He'd be furious, as morally offended as it was possible for a computer to be. And yet he'd understand Cassique's actions — or would *believe* he did. He'd see it as an example of long-dormant humanity rising to life, a misguided attempt to do good by the past. He'd send Cassique down without a second thought, but he wouldn't suspect anything else.

At least, that was what Cassique *hoped*.

Cassique flicked slowly through the rest of the papers, then looked idly over at the anxious applicant. He was an ordinary young man, the same as any other in Vienna. He had simple hopes and dreams, wanted no more than a good life and a middling career.

"You're not married, are you?" Cassique asked.

"Me? No," the boy gasped, and chuckled at the very idea.

"But there is a girl?" Cassique pressed, curious to know.

"One who is special, yes," the boy agreed.

"And you intend to marry her?"

"When I can afford it, yes, if she will have me."

Cassique nodded and studied the final drawing briefly before putting it to one side with the others. He scratched his chin and narrowed his eyes, giving the impression that he was considering a weighty matter and wasn't sure which way he'd swing. Finally, when he felt the act had gone on for long enough, he spoke.

"Very well, Master Hitler, we accept you."

Adolf's face lit up. "You do?"

"Yes. Your work is impressive. Rough around the edges, but we will help you iron out the creases during your stay here." Cassique offered his hand, and, after a pause, the newly enrolled art student accepted it. They shook hands and smiled, and Cassique found himself wondering what the world might have turned out like if this rewriting of history truly could have been.

Father caught up with him six jumps through time later. Five months Personal Time had passed, and he was beginning to worry that his tinkering with the young Adolf Hitler hadn't been detected.

Then he stepped down from his sky ship in the present to deliver his latest batch of Originals and there were six Fixers waiting for him, faces stern. He breathed a sigh of relief.

They took him, without saying a word, to a complex he'd never seen before. It was a small building, no different to any of the millions of others in the sprawling cities of Earth. They led him through the building, all the way to the back, where they entered an elevator. It dropped down eighteen levels, swiftly, smoothly. The doors slid open, and they escorted him into a large white room.

Five women sat behind the longest desk Cassique had ever seen. Nothing in their dress or make-up identified them as judges, but Cassique instinctively knew that was what they were.

His captors led him to a chair in the centre of the room. He sat without having to be directed and waited.

"You tried to change the true timeline, Cassique." The voice was Father's, a hologram of his head rising out of the middle of the desk as he spoke. Cassique looked aside guiltily but didn't otherwise respond. "Why?" Father asked.

"It's not right," Cassique said, still not meeting Father's gaze. "Millions died in the war because of that man. It's wrong that we let him push ahead and bring so much chaos, suffering, and death to the world."

"But how many billions from the following centuries would have died if we hadn't caught you in your treasonous attempt to alter the one true past?" Father asked.

"They wouldn't have died," Cassique countered, looking at Father directly now. "They'd have simply ceased to be when the Time Hole closed. It's not the same. We should use the Hole to change the past, to give humanity a chance of a better, brighter future."

"A Second World War of one sort or another would have happened regardless of Adolf Hitler's involvement," Father said. "Our experiments proved that long ago. Hitler happened to be the focal point in the original war, but events would have proceeded much as they did even without his presence as the leader of the National Socialist German Workers' Party."

"Perhaps," Cassique said, "but we can't be absolutely sure of that. I wanted to give the people of that time a chance."

Father mimicked a sigh and addressed the judges. "Ladies, he has admitted his guilt. He shows no signs of –"

"You can't go hitting me with a guilt trip!" Cassique yelled. "According to you, there are no laws anymore, and thus no crimes. How can I be guilty if there are no laws for me to break?"

"You are guilty of betraying Father." The central judge spoke the words. "You are guilty of betraying time. You are guilty of betraying every human being of the last nine hundred years. It's true, there are no longer officially recognised crimes or restrictive laws. Our ancestors decreed that Father should never be placed in a position where he was forced to pass judgement on humanity. That being the case, we, the chosen representatives of the human race, have been invested with the power to call for punishment in extreme situations, where we feel it is merited. You are guilty of no existing legal breaches, true, but there is a justice beyond legality."

"I've never heard of such a thing," Cassique snarled.

"It is beyond words," the judge said. "It is the law of the human heart, the human *soul*, if you will. You knew you were doing wrong when you went back and accepted Adolf Hitler's application to join the Academy of Fine Arts. Even though you broke no written laws, you *knew* you were doing wrong, didn't you?"

Cassique kept his lips tightly shut and didn't answer.

"Of course you knew," the judge continued. "You knew, because a force buried within you, a greater law than any of humanity's invented laws, told you so. Yet you went ahead and disobeyed that natural urging. For this you must be either punished or reconditioned."

"Reconditioned?" Cassique frowned.

"Your mind is diseased," the judge told him. "We can cure it, if you ask us."

"How?"

"Drugs. Surgery. Hypnotism. We have our ways."

"No." Cassique spat on the floor. "I won't live a lie. What we're doing in the past is wrong. Father is wrong. You are wrong. I won't be your puppet."

"You're sure of your words?" the judge asked. "Think carefully. If you reject reconditioning, you'll force us to punish you. We are not a cruel society, and always make the option of rebalancing available, even to the most heinous offenders such as yourself, but if you choose to follow this path…"

"Dos your reconditioning," Cassique growled.

"Very well," the judge said without any emotion. "In that case, you leave us no alternative. Are you prepared to receive the sentence of this court?"

"I thought we were beyond punishment," Cassique sneered. "Weren't punitive measures outlawed a few centuries back?"

"They were," the judge said.

"But you break that law anyway, right, to suit your own purposes. You make me sick. What is it — imprisonment? Torture? Banishment?"

"You have betrayed time," the judge said evenly. "Therefore, by time you shall be punished."

"You're going to beat me to death with a clock?" Cassique laughed.

"You will be punished just as all other offenders of your type are," the judge told him, ignoring his quip. "You'll be sent back through the past to a randomly selected time and place. Your mind will be altered before you go, as will your looks, to make you act in accordance with a specific role. You will then replace a figure of the past in their last moments."

"What?" Cassique acted confused. "I don't understand. What do you mean, *last moments*?"

"As a Gemini – which is what you now are from this moment forward – you will take the place of an Original in their dying moments," the judge explained. "For instance, you might end up in the Berlin bunker, in the last days of the war you were trying so hard to prevent, as the man you were trying to change — Adolf Hitler. You will know who you really are, but you won't be able to access your real self. Instead, you'll act as the Original did, speak as he did, follow the course he did, and kill yourself." The judge grinned tightly. "As your would-be student Adolf did."

"I'll *what*?" Cassique screamed. "Wait a minute! I've changed my mind! I'll take the personality switch. Give me the drugs and the scalpel."

"Too late," the judge said. "You had your chance, but it is gone. Father? A destination, please."

"That's not fair!" Cassique cried. "You didn't explain the rules. How can I be expected to choose fairly if I don't know the rules?"

"Ignorance is no excuse," the judge rumbled. "Listen and learn your fate."

Father's circuits whirred audibly for a few seconds, more for effect than any real reason, and then he produced the name Beta D had so cunningly arranged for him to unknowingly pick.

Suppressing the urge to smile, to beat the air with a triumphant fist and celebrate pulling the wool over the eyes of Father and his sycophantic judges, Cassique leapt to his feet and screamed. He tried lunging for the judges, as he'd seen criminals do in movies of the past, but the guards caught and subdued him before he could get further than a metre. Clasping his arms with their gloved hands — he saw their lips curl with distaste at having to make physical contact — and saying nothing at all, they led him away to another, much smaller room, where the preparations commenced.

Two days later his mind was no longer his own. As he was led to the time station, where he was to be launched back into the past to die a slow, painful death, he found himself gazing down at his altered body, watching his hands and feet as though they were somebody else's, which, in a way, they now were.

The sky ship was waiting for him. He'd hoped Chert would be there, so he could say farewell to his long-time colleague, but the two Fixers on duty were people he had never seen before.

His guards halted him at the entrance to the ship, and Father's projected face appeared in mid-air, level with Cassique's. He asked the guards to take a few steps back, then spoke softly, so that only Cassique could hear.

"I'm sorry to see you go like this," he said. "I know you might not believe me, that you have turned against me and think me a liar, but it's the truth. I care for all my children. I watch over them from the day of their birth to the day of their death and cherish every single one of them. If you had come to me and expressed your fears and doubts, I could have helped. I could have cured you."

Cassique wanted to tell him what he could do with his *cure*, but the restrictions of his conditioning prevented any reply.

"If you've been worrying about the Beta D and Albert Einstein Originals," Father went on, "you can relax. While I've no doubt they must have influenced your thinking in some warped way, they won't be punished for your crimes. They are not my children and not of our time, so they'll simply be kept immobile for the duration of their lives, safe and protected, unharmed. I cannot let them loose again, not after this fiasco. Indeed, I may have to consider restricting access to their later selves from now on." He was silent for a few seconds, mulling this over, then said, aloud to the guards, "Take him away." As they moved to obey his order, he added, to Cassique, "May your suffering be short."

The two Fixers led him into the ship, staring at him with mild curiosity. They didn't know about his crime or punishment. To them he was just another Gemini, going back to play out a role of his choosing. Cassique found himself wondering, as they led him to his chair, how many of the Geminis he had escorted to the past had actually gone there against their will. He'd only heard rumours of a few missing Fixers, but he was willing to bet there'd been a whole lot more that none of his contacts knew about.

As the sky ship rose into the air, he looked down upon his world for the final time. It nearly broke his heart, knowing he was leaving it forever. If he'd had his own voice, he would have had to fight with himself to stop it crying out for mercy, betraying his ambitions and plans. As it was, he said nothing, only stared down blankly and dumbly. He couldn't even force his hand to rise and wave goodbye.

Then the ship reached the prescribed level. The Fixers signalled their readiness to proceed with the mission. Shutters came down to cover the windows to protect the crew from the blinding light of the explosion, and the relevant molecules of matter, almost three thousand years old, were blasted against the ship's reactor.

And Cassique was off.

TEN

On July 2nd, 2862, having completed all temporal repairs, and satisfied that all the past timelines were as they should be, Father closed the Time Hole ahead of what would have been its natural collapse. It was marked in the calendars as a day of celebration and great cheer. Almost thirty percent of the people of the world tore themselves away from the sex spas and realities to bear witness to this end of an era.

Wherever people gathered, Father filled the skies with balloons, streamers, and fireworks. Tame entertainment compared with that of the realities, but quaintly nostalgic and mildly enjoyable for those in attendance.

The Fixers had all gathered in one place and were swapping stories about their travels into the past, the people they'd encountered, the places they'd visited. They were edgy, uneasy, though none would admit they were worried now that the Hole was closing, and their way of life was coming to an end.

Chert wasn't among hir colleagues. Having worked so many triple shifts in recent years, ze was sick of the past and had locked hirself away in hir favourite sex spa. Ze couldn't have cared less about the closure of the Time Hole and the final realignment of time. If this turned out to be the end of the world as they knew it, Chert was determined to blink out in grand, orgiastic style. Ze didn't even spare a thought for hir old pal Cassique, who, to the best of hir knowledge, had simply been reassigned to a different unit — Father had never told Chert anything about hir partner's betrayal and punishment.

Nijin and Zune met and greeted each other cordially. Many

ex-family units were reuniting, at Father's request, to lend an old-fashioned homely atmosphere to the proceedings.

A number of Originals had been taken out of holding for the day, including Cassique's Alb and Beta D, who were under strict supervision, and kept groggy and silent by drugs. Father wanted them there so they could see the route to the past vanishing, so they'd know that they were trapped here forever, no way back, captives of the one true present until the day they died.

As the moment of closure drew near, Father displayed a ten-second countdown on digital screens across the world. He encouraged his children to join him in the count, and dutifully they did. "Ten," they chanted in one huge global voice. "Nine. Eight. Seven. Six. Five. Four. Three. Two. One."

"We have –" Father began to announce.

Then the sky rippled, and the myriad pulsating lines of the Time Hole became visible to the naked eye for the first time ever. Everyone could see them vibrating and falling inwards, shattering, caving in, crushing all in their way.

In the briefest second before the white light blinded all, Alb and Beta D's gazes met, and their mouths creased into tiny, tired smirks.

Then the light covered the face of the globe and seared away the world of the present. Father disappeared in a flash, the Fixers, the crowds, Nijin and Zune, Chert, Beta D and Alb, the cities and seas and mountains and the monorail...

And the light swept backwards, wiping out every temporal reality it touched, streaking back through the layers of time, to 2700, 2600, 2500...

Back further, to the twentieth century, the 1700s, the Middle

Ages...

Back...

All the people and inventions and minds and buildings and voices and dreams and lands and visions and nations crumbled beneath the all-penetrating force of the light. All dissolved, all fell, all ceased to ever have been.

And back it continued, to the 900s, 600, 250, 100...

Back, back, back, all the way to 33 AD.

And then it stopped, suddenly, finally, and time began over anew. It started, inauspiciously enough, with a man nailed to a pair of crossed, wooden planks.

Cassique had been hanging on the cross for what seemed an eternity, though he knew it couldn't have been more than several hours.

He'd stepped in for the Original in the Garden, when all around were sleeping. The Fixers had left him there, whisked away the startled saviour, and he'd been ready and waiting when the guards arrived, when the traitor stepped up and kissed his cheek, completely unaware of his ironic mistake.

Cassique had automatically gone along with the recorded version of events until this moment, suffering the slings and blows and harsh words, saying only what the Book had reported. This was in accordance with their plan. They had to make it look genuine. Fixers would be monitoring him all the way to the cross, to make sure his programming didn't fail, but they'd depart once he was up there, and wouldn't check back for a couple of decades. If he could change the words whilst on the cross, just slightly...

According to the Book, the Original had delivered a lengthy monologue, which had included a couple of his trademark parables. Cassique, Alb, and Beta D had cut out a lot of this, though they'd kept the bones of it intact. In its place they'd prepared a shorter, snappier speech, largely the same in spirit, but altered enough so that it should do the required job.

In his mind, fighting to overcome the unimaginable pain, Cassique uttered the words which would override Father's conditioning and make way for Alb's and Beta D's. He felt the mental walls crumble as he did so, the orders of the first planted layer overriding those of the second, and he breathed raggedly and moved his lips, for the first time in this long and testing trip, of his own accord.

He opened his eyes and looked down on the barren world of the past, the weeping women, the jeering crowd. He tried forcing his mouth to deliver the speech, but to his horror found he was too tired to make it work. He could clearly see the words he'd memorised, swimming around before his eyes, but he couldn't force his beaten, battered body to reach out and pluck them from the air.

He struggled valiantly for a couple of hours, repeating the words to himself, gathering his strength, concentrating, working his tongue from left to right in an attempt to free it, but every time he tried to open his mouth and speak, he failed. It was too much. His lips were cracked and bleeding. The sun was burning his brain to mush. His muscles were weak and throbbing and screaming for release. All he really wanted to do was die. All he felt ready for was death.

Eventually he abandoned the fight and relaxed. He had done

all he could. He had tried. Maybe his not saying anything would be enough. Perhaps the Fixers wouldn't notice when they returned and would leave things be. Shaking his head slowly, weeping, he prayed to a god he'd never believed in for strength. His people needed him to be strong, to succeed. He might destroy them in doing so, but their time would come again, their age would dawn once more. And maybe this time things would happen differently, and they wouldn't throw all their eggs into the one computer-lined basket, wouldn't waste their lives on virtual games and sex spas, wouldn't make aliens of their fellow human beings, wouldn't come back and exploit the past, and they'd remember what it meant to be human...

His head lifted slowly, and he spoke. He didn't know he was speaking until he had finished. The words came of their own accord, from a source deep down, from what the people of the past would have perhaps called his soul, and he died, not long after that, not remembering what he had said, not knowing if his death had had meaning or not.

"Father," he'd murmured, referring to those of his own present, who had given away so much, who had stripped their world of its human qualities, and allowed a computer to steal their children and reduce them to the level of easily distracted buffoons, "forgive them. They know not what they do."

And with that, the die of the future was cast.

Amen.

I wrote the first draft of this book some time in the 1990s.

I finished my final edit on the 27th of July 2023.

I think it's rather apt that it travelled so far through time with me!

For all those who are working in their own small way to make the world of the Future a better place.

Darren Dash, 21st september 2023.

Printed in Great Britain
by Amazon

fb195b6c-c728-4c19-8751-87e7f7606921R01